Trouble is coming," she said to the man before her.

"Yes, there is no way to prevent it."

"But they must not find this place," she worried. . . .

". . . the evil ones must not know where this cottage is."

Note for Librarians: A cataloguing record for this book is available from Library and Archives Canada at www.collectionscanada.ca/amicus/index-e.html
ISBN 1-4120-6074-5

Printed in Victoria, BC, Canada. Printed on paper with minimum 30% recycled fibre.
Trafford's print shop runs on "green energy" from solar, wind and other environmentally-friendly power sources.

TRAFFORD
PUBLISHING™
Offices in Canada, USA, Ireland and UK

Book sales for North America and international:
Trafford Publishing, 6E–2333 Government St.,
Victoria, BC V8T 4P4 CANADA
phone 250 383 6864 (toll-free 1 888 232 4444)
fax 250 383 6804; email to orders@trafford.com
Book sales in Europe:
Trafford Publishing (UK) Limited, 9 Park End Street, 2nd Floor
Oxford, UK OX1 1HH UNITED KINGDOM
phone 44 (0)1865 722 113 (local rate 0845 230 9601)
facsimile 44 (0)1865 722 868; info.uk@trafford.com
Order online at:
trafford.com/05-0975

10 9 8 7 6 5 4

MARTEN RIVER HIDEAWAY

ANNE RAVENOAK

House of RavenOak

In partnership with

TRAFFORD PUBLISHING

THIS BOOK IS FOR

Elsie Tomkins

Who was in at the very beginning of this little adventure and will remain always in my fondest memories.

And for her daughter, Carolyn Tomkins-White, who has her mom's loving heart.

Acknowledgments

Thank you to my support group: Readers: Helen Curlook, Jean York, Marguerite Zilz, Kerri Tipler, Kathleen Burgess, and to Kim Tipler, Maria Maille, Bonnie Houston, Marisa Maille, Suzanne Harmony and, as always, HG, *the wind beneath my wings.*

Cover Art and Design: **Kim Tipler**
Edited by: **Kathleen Burgess**

CHAPTER ONE

Dysfunctional family--that was the cause of her problems according to the latest psychotherapist. Jade pondered this pronouncement as she smoothly handled her red sports car. She drove as though the police were still after her, thoughts roving chaotically, latching onto the landscape, grounding themselves. Now that she was out of the Toronto traffic and past Barrie and Orillia, the highway became one long winding track. Massive rock, pines and tamarack abutted the highway on both sides. Her mind, with little to distract it, wandered to the past.

"Why?" she had asked him. He was one of a long line of professionals she had consulted in the past few months to help clear up the disaster that was her life. Why did she fail in relationships? Why did she keep getting involved with lowlifes? Why did she keep having visions of unreality? Why couldn't her life run smoothly, the way the lives of her friends seemed to? *Seemed* was the key word here. After all, she knew that to her friends, her life seemed perfect too.

She sighed as she negotiated a particularly tricky curve in Highway 11. Now that she was past Huntsville, she breathed deeply, inhaling the invigorating pine-pungent air. "You can always tell when you arrive in the north country," she had told Bernie, her employer. "The air changes. It becomes scented with the pines, the earth, the wildness. Especially at night." She had needed this holiday, needed to get away to her aunt's cottage, tucked away in the bush in Marten River. She had phoned her aunt in Florida, asking Kate for permission to use her cottage for a few days. The nonchalance she had forced when she talked to her aunt was a sham. Aunt Kate wouldn't want to hear about this latest escapade in her niece's short troubled life.

"Should I come home, Jade?" Her aunt had worried. "Do you need someone to talk to?" But Jade had assured her that she would be all right on her own. "I know you will, Dear. You always come through in the end, you know. You're a survivor."

If you only knew, thought Jade. *I'm probably more of a survivor than even you suspect, Kate.* She was very fond of her aunt, having gone to her often in her trouble-laden youth for moral support when she couldn't handle the situation at home. Her aunt had advised her long ago to move away from her parents, to take charge of her own life. However, in the end, there had been no need.

First, her mother had taken her own life, unable to find the strength to change her pattern of living. Then her father had drunk himself into oblivion and willed himself to die within a few months of her mother. It was a case, Jade mused, of not being able to live together or apart. She remembered her twentieth birthday when her father had died, and it seemed she had been confused and searching ever since. For what, she didn't know.

She and Kate had both known that it would not have worked out with Jade living with her aunt. Each needed her own privacy. But Kate had always been there for her when she needed it. It was Kate who had talked her into going to college to develop skills to help her be independent. That had proven to be as excellent a piece of advice as Jade had ever received. True, she hadn't become proficient in using her journalism degree yet, but she had sold a few pieces of freelance work.

Maybe I'm growing up, Jade thought. She didn't need her aunt now; she just needed her aunt's cottage so that she could escape from the latest mess in Toronto. Why hadn't she clued in that Derek had been selling cocaine and even harder drugs? How had he kept that side of his life so hidden from her? It wasn't until Jade had begun to question some of his late-night visitors and his nightly meetings that he had evasively answered some of her questions.

He had been the man of her dreams since she had met him in the book store where she worked part time for Bernie. The minute he had walked into the store looking for a crime adventure book, she had fallen head over heels in love with him. She had trembled as she directed him to one of her favorite authors, who wrote about espionage and international intrigue. Most of the people she knew who liked this type of novel were happy to live vicariously for a few hours. For the most part, their lives were ones of routine--an average job, average home, average kids. For a short while they could infiltrate the minds of criminals and police officers, maverick spies and renegade cops. Once the reader closed the book, he or she would settle back into the reality of life. By the time Derek had selected a specific book, she was already smitten--dark blond wavy hair, grey eyes, tanned skin, and slim, athletic body. He no more fit her preconceived image of a drug dealer than her aunt did.

Their relationship had started off slowly at first. With the visual acuity of hindsight, she acknowledged that she had acted more like a teenage groupie than a twenty-five-year-old university graduate holding down two part-time jobs. Now that she thought about it, it was more reluctance on his part than on hers to become so involved. "Well, that was one good point Derek had going for him," she mused aloud, as CBC radio poured out the Hallelujah chorus from Handel's Messiah. He really hadn't wanted to involve her in his activities. Now that she could think back to the past few months with a degree of objectivity, she realized that she had been the one to push the relationship.

She shuddered, thinking about it, and wished she had brought one of her friends along on this trip, so she wouldn't have had time to think. But she hadn't, and her thoughts took wing on their own.

The police had been reluctant to believe that she had taken no part in that aspect of Derek's life. It had taken much pleading, and a considerable number of good words from her friends to persuade the police that she knew nothing. She wondered how she could have been so naive.

As she continued to drive automatically, mulling over the last few months, the day wore on toward late afternoon. Jade eased off the accelerator, keeping well below the speed limit on the new bypass. The hills, valleys, and rocks of Huntsville had given way gradually to the rolling farm land of the Powassan area. There were hills in the distance, but the land was gentler somehow, more appealing to her senses. It seemed very much like the English countryside as Jade remembered it from a trip she had taken when she was about twelve, as part of her aunt's extended family. What she hadn't actually seen, she had conjured in her imagination from the many books she read.

"You're too much of a dreamer, young Jade," Bernie had said many times.

For some reason, Jade had been able to confide in him almost to the point that she could confide in her aunt. Maybe she looked on him as a surrogate father--an archetypal Jewish father dispensing sage advice. Outwardly he filled the bill for a patriarchal biblical figure. She wasn't so sure Bernie would see himself that way. Both the older people recognized the void in her life, perceived the searching that was the primal force of her existence. Even Jade herself didn't see it for what it was--a search for a place to belong.

After her episode with Derek, which had devastated her, she realized that she had never really loved him at all. If so, she reasoned, she would have stuck by him, no matter what. Instead, she had dropped him immediately, appalled by his drug involvement. She had been dismayed by the fact that he had been hiding part of his life from her until the police had confronted him in her presence. "Just trying to protect you, Kid," he had said. He had always called her *Kid*, never Jade, now that she thought about it. On his side, she had been simply someone to confide in now and then when he had felt like confiding, and she was someone who idolized him. She had craved the relationship, but he had not needed it--had not even wanted the adulation she had bestowed upon him.

After Derek, Jade had taken her aunt's long-standing advice and put herself into therapy. *I've got to find out*, she had worried, *what it is about me, what it is that gets me into these messes.* It was not only her relationships that concerned her, but also the visions that beset her. After several long therapy sessions, she had finally come to acknowledge that what the therapist said had some merit. He had told her that she was searching for stability. She was searching for a relationship in which she could feel comfortable and secure.

"Most people more or less goes through the same searching," her therapist had told her. "But in children from dysfunctional families, the search is intensified. Usually, these adult children cannot relate properly to their peers or to older people. They view the world differently because of their upbringing, or lack of it, to be more precise."

That theory was all well and good. *But it doesn't do much to help me.* Jade grimaced and inhaled sharply as she barely missed a brown deer that had come perilously close to the near-deserted highway. She could cope fairly well, thanks, just by being aware of what she was doing and why. In this respect, the sessions had helped her, but other than that, she felt she was strong enough to manage on her own.

The last therapist had skillfully avoided discussing her visions. She was well aware of the way people backed off when anything like ESP was mentioned, and she was resigned to letting the topic slide when she noted their unease.

Just as she drew up to a set of traffic lights at the entrance to Northgate Square, she tossed her moon-blond hair back off her face. Green eyes glanced into the rearview mirror, surveying the traffic in all directions. Not much farther to go. The small city of North Bay seemed to have grown since she had been through last. It had been four years since she had visited her aunt's cottage; four years since her Aunt Kate had given up her house in North Bay and moved to Florida to escape the cold winter that the area often experienced. Not really cold, though, not nearly as debilitating as people farther south seemed to think, but sometimes prolonged. The area moved from winter to summer in one fell swoop of glory. Diehard outdoor enthusiasts were hard pressed to get their winter toys cleaned and stored before boating and fishing started.

The city was moving ahead at a vigorous pace. This information had come in one of her aunt's letters. Kate still kept her cottage at Marten River, but only because Jade had turned down Kate's generous offer of the cottage as her own. When Kate had told her she could have it, Jade had demurred. Kate had her own family--two daughters and a son. True, Kate would see them taken care of, but Jade had felt they should have the cottage, too. She had told her aunt this in one of their frequent conversations.

"But, Jade, you make more use of the cottage than do my three put together. They quite understand, so you needn't feel guilty."

"I don't," Jade had replied. "Your three, Aunt Kate, haven't needed the cottage as a bolt hole, as I have."

As the traffic started forward, Jade thought back to the conversation that had taken place six years ago when she had celebrated her twentieth birthday, just a short time after her father had given up, and she had found herself alone.

"Yes, I know, Jade. I wish I could have done more for you," Aunt Kate had continued, with tears in her eyes. "I did want you to come and live with me when you were younger, but your mother wouldn't let you."

"I remember, Aunt. I probably wouldn't have come anyway. I always felt that Mom needed me to look after her, to be a defense against Dad. Now that I'm able to look back from a distance, I can see that she didn't need me as an intermediary. The strangest thing is, I still loved them, even with their drinking and their inability to function as mature adults. Between the drinking bouts, they were model parents, except that by that time, they didn't have a model child. I guess children who grow up in alcoholic homes are so used to being the responsible person, it's hard for them to go back to being a child in between times, and they revert to childlike behavior in adulthood." Over the intervening years, Jade had tried to stop blaming herself for her parents' problems, knowing that each person is responsible for his or her own life.

Intellectually she knew that. Emotionally, she sometimes had trouble accepting the fact. She still had to overcome her own shortcomings as she saw them, had to learn to cope with the world around her so that both she and the world would come out winners. *As it is,* she mused as she moved with the traffic, *I am still in the battle with the outcome undecided.* Well, at least she was still in there fighting. She gave herself credit for that.

Pressing down lightly on the accelerator, she guided the car smoothly through the intersection. No need to speed up yet; the next set of traffic lights at Trout Lake Road and the Bypass would be coming up in two blocks. After Trout Lake Road, she drove four kilometers until she was able to exit onto the north ramp, then up Thibeault Hill between the red granite rocks, and she was truly northward bound. She breathed deeply, sinking further into the cream-colored leather upholstery and willing a bone-deep tension out of her body. Amid turquoise and tangerine wisps of cloud, the sun had set over a brooding Lake Nipissing. The dense forest closed around her as she continued her drive. The rampant growth of the bush held no horrors for her. From childhood, it had offered a sanctuary from her problems and had comforted her when she needed an escape. Little did she know that the mysterious northern bush was again to play an extremely important role in her life.

This was where she longed to have her dream cottage someday. It was not Aunt Kate's cottage; of that she was certain. Her ideal was more along the lines of the European cottages she had dreamed about from childhood. Could you put an English cottage in the Canadian bush? Or would it be incongruous? She had seen how some immigrants had tried to re-create their homelands in this new country. It didn't work. Was she trying to do the same thing? Trying to impose an old lifestyle onto a new situation? Acculturation was the key.

One had to adapt to new surroundings. This was where her parents had become lost. They had not been able to adapt. They had clung desperately to their past, fearing to hold it lightly, and in doing so, fit in nowhere. She felt that this had been the basis for their problems. They had resorted to a slow death through alcohol as a way to forget, unable to move forward, ashamed to look back.

Alone on the deserted highway, she had her thoughts to keep her company. There was another reason she had not wanted Aunt Kate to deed her the vacation property. She had not told Aunt Kate, but she surmised that her aunt had guessed anyway. Although Jade used her aunt's cottage quite extensively, she still did not feel entirely at ease there. Aunt Kate's cottage had a rustic log exterior and pine interior. Jade knew that if she had the cottage, she could change it to suit herself, but she felt that this would be a travesty of the very essence that made it such a haven, as it was. But even more than the construction, there was a new malignant quality about the cottage that escaped Jade's analysis. It hadn't always been there. She had noticed it the last time she came up. If this had been five years ago, she would have found deep comfort in the cottage. No, the creeping baseness had entered stealthily, silently in the past few years.

What was it that Carlos Castaneda had written? People have definite places where they feel comfortable, where everything comes together for them. The ancient art of Feng Shui considered the same concept. Everything in the universe has its rightful place. And when everything is in its right place, soul and body come together in harmony. Two different philosophies, two worlds apart, thought the same way. So there must be something to it. Well, her aunt's cottage had been close to it, but not quite. It was not the dream cottage of her vision. No, her cousins should have the cottage, and their children could make use of it. She would find her own place. She knew exactly what she wanted. This holiday would be a good time to look for it. Her friend Jean from Re/Max had been looking for one for her, but to no avail.

"What you want, Jade, is in your head, not out there being sold," Jean had finally told her in an exasperated voice. "You're looking for something that exists on the other side of the rainbow, or in a fairy tale book. Accept the fact that you will have to buy an overpriced house in the suburbs, or maybe even a condo.

"You're not going to find your English country garden house anywhere near where you work, unless you go to England." Jean was blunt, and Jade appreciated her friend's attempt to bring her back to earth. That didn't stop the longing, though. For all her forthrightness, however, Jean was soft-hearted. Although she tried to get Jade to see reality, Jean would keep trying to find her a cottage that she could afford, in an area in which she could find work. It was Jean's empathy with her clients that made her a top Re/Max real estate salesperson and one of Jade's closest friends.

Jade was lost in thought and musings as she soared along the highway. A blue Buick Skylark with SULLI licence plates dashed past her. With little traffic it was easy to surpass the speed limit, she reflected. Now paying little attention to her own driving, she too pressed her foot down more heavily on the accelerator, releasing the cruise control.

Sunshine Lane was left behind in a flash; the neatly groomed lawns of the psychiatric hospital blurred on her right. In no time she was out of the North Bay area and nearing Tomiko Restaurant. Suddenly out of the dusky twilight, she saw a red light flashing behind her. Jolted out of her reverie, Jade slowed the car and pulled over onto the graveled shoulder just past a sign announcing **Tomiko Lake 36.7 Km.**

Belatedly, she realized that she had been speeding, but still she was not concerned. The man, dressed in casual dark clothes, unfolded his tall frame from his unmarked car and approached her. Jade rolled the window down part way. Already she was miffed at the unsportsmanlike way by which he had caught her.

"Good evening, Miss." His deep voice reverberated along the long expanse of road, commanding the darkening shadows back into the bush. "You were driving pretty fast. May I see your license please." It wasn't a question, Jade noted. More of a demand. She decided he was unapproachable and slightly arrogant. He was trying to put on a macho act, believing his car and red light and his tall, muscular frame gave him authority and power. He acted as though he were wearing a uniform. That he wasn't, annoyed her all the more. She rummaged through her handbag, tossing aside tissues, lip balm, tampons, headache pills. Finally she fingered the small plastic case where she kept her licence and insurance. Jade knew all about police officers, having had the experience with Derek and the drug trafficking. Nevertheless, knowing that she had done nothing seriously wrong this time, she decided it would be in her best interests to cooperate.

"You were going thirty kilometers over the speed limit," the voice intoned. "I've been watching you for the past twenty kilometers."

Jade looked skeptically into the deep black eyes, trying frantically not to get lost in their fathomless depths. "What?" She was outraged. She had never gone thirty kilometers over the speed limit in her life, and told him so.

"Maybe you just didn't realize it," the officer spoke softly, obviously trying to placate her. "It's quite easy to speed when you're on a deserted highway. The problem in this area is that the highway just might not be deserted," he continued, as though he were addressing a teenager. She eyed him belligerently and took a deep breath, intending to break into his sermon. As she inhaled, a masculine scent of Pine River cologne and male sweat flowed into her lungs and stopped her short.

If not cars, then she could quite easily hit a moose that might wander out to the highway to get away from the blackflies in the bush. His voice drifted in and out of her consciousness as her senses reeled. "True, the moose might be killed," he pressed his argument, pointing at the same time to a yellow moose crossing sign about four meters ahead. "But you could just as easily be killed yourself, especially traveling at the speed you were." He was unaware of the effect he was having on her.

She looked at him scathingly. He didn't have to condescend to her, the chauvinist. She knew this area well. He was treating her as he would treat a tourist from the city. Well, she was from the city, but there were extenuating circumstances which she would like him to know about. The fact that she had silently castigated the driver of the Buick when it had passed her only a few minutes earlier didn't register. She swallowed. She knew that she had often gone twenty kilometers over the speed limit, and although she had never noticed herself going any faster than that, it was just possible that she might have. However, she wasn't about to let him off that easily. "Why didn't you go after that dark blue Buick that passed me?" She admonished him innocently.

Not answering her question directly, he said in a soft-spoken accent that she found difficult to place, "Tell you what, I'll let you go this time, but if I see you speeding again, it will be a ticket for sure." He had noticed her Toronto address on her licence and felt sure that he would never see her again. Why this should bother him, he didn't understand. "Where are you headed in such a hurry, anyway?" he asked. For some reason he wanted to keep her talking. In the gathering darkness he could see that she was apprehensive and ticked off, but trying to hide it.

"I'm going to my aunt's cottage, just this side of Marten River," she told him. Although she wanted to add that it was none of his business, discretion prevented her from uttering the words. "And I'm trying to get there before it gets too dark. I'm quite familiar with this area," she added for emphasis.

"I would really appreciate it if you would just give me a ticket, or let me go, so that I can continue. I promise I will keep an eye on the speedometer, and on my foot," she bubbled. She, too, was torn between the desire to get to her destination and a reluctance to leave this bulwark of male chauvinism who was capable of making her feel protected and arousing her antagonism at the same time. Maybe, she shuddered lightly, he represented something human and warm in this vast forest of trees and rocks. Perhaps he represented a human presence that she very much needed, however much she had been fleeing from people before this moment.

"How far is the cottage?" He leaned against her window, trying to stave off the moment of leaving. "Just about fifteen kilometers." She explained to him where the cottage was situated. "Ah, yes, I know the place. Not used very much. Okay, but remember not to speed." He didn't tell her he had no authority in this jurisdiction and no way of writing a ticket if he had. He was just as much a visitor here as she was, even if this had been his home for all the years of his childhood and youth.

After she had started her car and he returned to his, he wondered about her and about his reaction. Why had he stopped her? Why did he find himself attracted to her? At thirty-six, he was not a young teenager bursting for a quick rut in the back seat of a car. He had satisfied his sexual urges with women before. Not that many, but a few for whom his former uniform had acted as a turn on. When it got down to the serious business of a committed relationship, he found that they could not accept that he was a human being, flaws and all. Not seeing beyond the police uniform, they had placed him on a pedestal.

When he inevitably fell off, none of the women with whom he thought he could have a relationship could accept his fall from the imposed height. Even his wife of years ago had not been able to accept that he, too, was a person in need of warmth and closeness. He couldn't deny that he liked the macho image he exuded, but there were times, especially during difficult cases, when *he* needed the ego stroking, or even just someone to listen.

He had been troubled for a long time, thinking that there was something terribly wrong with him. Why couldn't he have a lasting relationship? One of his friends had half jokingly told him that he fell for the wrong women. "You fall for the soft, kittenish ways that women use around you," Tom had said.

Women wanted his masculinity, needed it. And for the most part he could satisfy them. But at the times he needed the comforting, his esteem boosted, the relationship invariably died.

She had pulled her red sports car back onto the road and continued on her way. For ten minutes he followed her at some distance, to check to see if she speeded up again, he told himself, seeing for a moment those haunting sea-green eyes and moon-gold hair. Somewhere deep down, he knew that he was following to see that she arrived safely at her cottage. A few kilometers down the road--it wasn't fifteen as she had said--she pulled off into a bush road on the left. He knew that the cottage was close to the road, but it was hidden in a copse of maple and birch.

As he drove by and slowed his speed, he noticed she had let herself in and had turned on the electric lights, one on the outside and one in a room in the cottage. She seemed to be okay for the time being, but caught unawares he found himself wrestling with a soul-deep uneasiness. He would check on her again tomorrow, he decided. He had failed to ask her how long she would be staying, but knew he could remedy that oversight the next day with a few casual and judicious questions. Feeling only a little relieved, he pressed down on the accelerator and drove further north to his destination.

Jade had indeed turned on two lights in the cottage, frowning as she wondered why no one had flipped off the main breaker switch. The sight that met her eyes dismayed and shocked her. A broken pane of glass from the kitchen window gave evidence that the cottage had been broken into sometime earlier. Subsequently, the forest animals, most especially squirrels and chipmunks, and from the look of the droppings scattered about, a platoon of deer mice, had found their way into her sanctuary and caused havoc. She glanced quickly about the rooms. There seemed to be no ransacking of the place, so destruction had not been the intent of the intruders. Probably, she decided, someone had needed a place to stay for the night and had broken the window to gain entrance. No, it had to be the debris and chaos caused by the animals that gave the cottage its musty, dirty air and caused the small hairs on the back of her neck to bristle.

She considered this as she flipped the switch for the pump to fill the water tank and turned on the hot water heater. She wasn't afraid of the squirrels, birds, or chipmunks that might have made their way in through the broken window, so she couldn't pinpoint the exact cause of the frisson of fear that traveled down her back.

She felt too tired to clean that night, but she did manage to pull the top of an old Hoosier cupboard over the broken window, hoping that would keep out any stray animals and blackflies for the night. She knew she could return to North Bay the next day to buy a pane of glass to replace the broken one. In the meantime, she pulled a set of clean sheets from a suitcase. She always carried her own set with her, knowing that if there were any in the cottage, they would be musty from disuse and dampness. She was especially glad of her foresight this night, when she suspected that any number of people or things might have slept in the cottage since the window had been broken.

Going into the bathroom she saw that it was just as messy as the rest of the house. Fortunately there was nothing wrong with the water supply, but she did run the tap for several minutes to clear the pipes of stale water. It was too soon for hot water, but by morning she would have lots. After rinsing in the cold water, Jade returned to the bedroom, made up the bed and fell into it. She didn't even have time to dwell on her problems before she dropped off into a deep sleep, void of any dreams except one. She was being chased through the bush by a tall dark cop.

Early next morning, Jade awoke to the sounds of the bush. She loved this time of day. Her sleep had refreshed her, and she stretched her long limbs and felt like she thought a contented cat would feel when it stretched after catnapping in a bed of cat mint. Through the unbroken but dusty bedroom window, she could hear robins. Somewhere a blue jay squawked, and shy warblers, camouflaged in the leafy trees, trilled cheerily. Her mind floated for a few moments on the medley of bird song.

Forcing herself out of bed, Jade scuffed to the window. The lemon-yellow morning sun, still pale in the blue sky, shone into the small clearing. The ferns and jewelweed glistened with thousands of multicolored diamonds in the soft light.

As she yawned and stretched some more to get the kinks out of muscles unused to the mattress, a black squirrel dashed across the weed-strewn yard in an early morning hunt for nuts and pine cones. A perky chipmunk chattered and clicked in the overgrown garden. She turned her attention to the shabbiness of the place. The yard and cottage had certainly been neglected in the past few years. No wonder intruders felt secure breaking in. Probably no one connected to Aunt Kate had been close to the cottage since she and Kate had closed it four years ago.

She often wondered why Aunt Kate's own children had no use for the cottage. Surely she wasn't the only one to have problems from which she felt a periodic need to escape. *But,* she grimaced to herself, *I seem quite adept at getting into more trouble and having more problems than anyone else I know.* A self-deprecating smile crossed her face. Already, her cares were beginning to lose their sharp edge. The north always helped her that way.

It was the surrounding bush, as much as anything. Jade certainly couldn't say that it was the cottage itself, especially in its present disreputable state. Pushing herself away from the window, she went in search of some of the food she had brought with her. She would make herself a leisurely breakfast, she promised herself, and then she would tackle the filth of the place. As contented as she was beginning to feel, however, she could not erase two ephemeral images that continued to lurk in the periphery of her mind. The one was the annoyingly smug police officer of the previous night, and the other was the vulnerability she now felt because her once-safe refuge had suffered intrusion. Which caused her the more disquiet, she couldn't have said.

CHAPTER TWO

First things first, Jade reminded herself as she scrubbed the well-worn Formica-topped kitchen counter with a bleach solution. She scrounged for bread in the cardboard box and made toast and coffee, her regular city breakfast, then added bacon and eggs, her holiday and weekend menu. When she had eaten a leisurely meal, she climbed into her beloved car, debating with herself whether to drive north to the Tri Towns or return to North Bay to purchase the new pane of glass. Before breakfast, she had carefully measured the window and sketched a diagram to make the job of glass buying easier. More familiar with the area of North Bay, she opted for the larger town as the most likely place to carry replacement glass.

She took her time driving back along the highway, noting with satisfaction the pleasant changes in the scenery from the night before. Now that the early morning sun was shedding its rays over the countryside, the bushes and trees glowed with a warmth like the ads for coffee that wash the picture in a golden haze.

As she was nearing the city, the figure of the police officer of the night before again intruded into her reverie. *He has a way of doing that*, she thought, with an irritated toss of her hair, inclined to blame him instead of her wayward thoughts. His image had stared at her from the dusty bedroom window, had smirked up at her from her cup of coffee, and had eyed her suspiciously from the newly-scrubbed kitchen counter. She was still thinking of him when she neared Cedar Heights Drive and decided to drive by the university to view any changes that had occurred in her absence.

Cruising slowly by the modern structure, she noticed the new additions. The building had doubled in size and now bore more resemblance to a big city campus. She then drove down College Drive and was surprised to see a new Ontario Provincial Police station at the bottom of the hill. Up to that point she had entertained no plans to report the damaged cottage window. Now she found herself flicking on her signal and turning into the police station parking lot. She hoped she wouldn't have to encounter the patronizing man from the previous night. Almost in the same thought was the picture of him in his casual clothes, and she wondered what he would look like in a dark blue uniform.

She had resented the high-handed manner with which he had stopped her and hoped she wouldn't meet up with him again, but synchronous with this resentment was a petulance because she had hoped he would stop by the cottage to see if she was all right, and he hadn't done that. She vacillated between the two contradictory emotions, acknowledging the polar discrepancy with a wry smile as she found the front door and entered the building.

Her long, jean-clad legs had a volition all their own as they strode purposefully to the desk. She spoke to the man she presumed to be in charge. He was bent over the desk poring over a girly magazine, or maybe it was police reports, she wasn't sure which. Since the episode in Toronto, her notion of a hard-working, honest-to-the-core police department had become a little tarnished.

"Excuse me." Her voice sounded raspy from the dust lying about the cottage.

The young middle-aged man looked up eagerly, awaiting any new events that might suspend the boredom of his job. He smiled politely and approached the desk. "Well, good morning, Miss. What can I do for you?" His tone implied he was expecting something as mundane as car trouble or a request for directions. He regarded her with undisguised appreciation. She looked good in her jeans and a pink Stratford Festival sweatshirt.

Noticing that he spoke with the soft drawl of someone who had been raised in the north country, she explained to him about the broken window of her aunt's cottage. He stared at her for a moment, then pulled a form towards him. She thought he seemed to take the matter more seriously than it warranted.

"Would you like a cup of coffee while you fill this out?" he asked, as he handed her a form. "I've just made it, so it's fresh." He grinned at her.

She longed to say *yes*, but she shook her head. "No thanks. I'm in a hurry to get back to clean the cottage so I can enjoy the rest of my stay."

"Like it here, do you?" he enquired, seemingly interested.

"I like the area; my aunt has always been more than kind to lend her cottage to me on short notice. She offered to give it to me, but somehow I didn't feel right accepting it," Jade continued, wondering all the while why she was so forthcoming with her information and whether her reaction was a result of her recent episode with the Toronto police.

"Hmm, I know what you mean."

The cop looked like a typical family man, Jade decided, as she openly regarded him. Nothing startlingly handsome about him, not like the officer of the evening before, but he was fairly good looking. Right now he looked rather tired and a little cynical and bored. He may not be as good looking as the guy who stopped her, but he didn't look anywhere near as smug either, she noted with some asperity.

"I would like to call in Detective Sergeant McKechnie from Toronto," he said, in a manner that told her he would do just that whether Jade agreed or not.

"Why is this such a big deal?" she asked, somewhat puzzled. "It's a simple broken window. Nothing was taken, as far as I know. But I will call Aunt Kate in Florida to tell her what happened."

He seemed reluctant to tell her anything more, but asked, "You're staying there alone?" She immediately recognized the noncommittal tone. She hadn't gone through the inquisition in Toronto without learning a few things about cops.

"Yes," Jade replied for what she was sure was the fourth or fifth time. "Look, I've looked after myself for years. I'm not worried, and no, I don't think anyone will come gunning for me in the night. Although I do write, my writing is factual and I'm not given to having morbid fanciful thoughts," she informed him. Even so, she felt the same small ripple of fear that she had felt earlier. She quickly shrugged it off. The unknown was usually worse than the actual event itself. Just as she was readjusting her thinking, the outside door through which she had entered, opened.

"Jay!" The sergeant behind the desk looked up in surprise. "I didn't expect to see you in this area for another couple of days, at least. When I called TO to see if you would like to come up for a visit, I didn't expect you to drop everything."

The newcomer laughed. "When you say `Come up for a visit,' Tom, it means that you have something you would like me to help you with, off the record, that is."

Jade, filling in the form, bristled at the familiar voice. She looked up just in time to see the handsome, arrogant officer she had encountered the night before.

"Jason, this is Jade..."

"...Morgan." Jade supplied her last name as Tom, ever on the lookout for his friend's love life, made the introductions. So, the bigshot was the detective from Toronto that the sergeant had wanted to notify.

"Jason and Jade," Tom commented, looking at the two of them with a mischievous twinkle in his eyes. "Nice-sounding as a couple, don't you think, Jay?" A look, which Jade couldn't identify, passed between the two old friends.

She tried to ignore the man from Toronto. He was such a supercilious beast, everything she detested in a man.

"I think we met last night." Jade's sea-green eyes met his obsidian ones. "Officer McKechnie or Detective McKechnie or whatever," she sniffed haughtily, "pulled me off to the side last night and informed me I was speeding." She ended with some surliness.

He smiled grimly. "You *were* speeding. "I would hate to see your pretty neck hanging at a crooked angle amid wreckage in a ditch or against a rock-cut or a tree," he snarled. "Moose don't think ahead to the consequences of a collision. But maybe I shouldn't care. Maybe I should just let you do it."

She was startled by the animosity emanating from him.

Tom looked quizzically at his friend. "Whoa.... This isn't like you, Jay."

Jason and Jade looked at each other. Whereas she had an annoyed look, his was positively hostile. She had no way of knowing that after their meeting the previous evening, he had phoned Toronto and had her run through the computerized identification program. He couldn't even have said what had made him do it. Maybe it was self-preservation, maybe it was gut reaction. What he found out had dismayed him. She didn't look the type to be involved in drugs. She looked too innocent, too vulnerable. True, she had been cleared of any involvement in the dealings, but the information had still troubled him more than it should have. He didn't understand his feelings himself, but shrugged them off, refusing to analyze them.

When he had followed her last night, he had observed

her pulling something dark and heavy across the window to obscure the light so no one from the highway would notice that the cottage was occupied. Now, he said cryptically to her, "How's Derek?"

Jade blanched and a cold sweat burst upon her forehead. Was it always going to be like this? she wondered. Was her life going to be one of suspicion from now on, simply because she had fallen for the wrong man? She didn't want Jason or the nice sergeant behind the desk to notice that she was upset, but she surmised that being a detective, Jason had noticed anyway. Just like a doctor. They always seemed to notice things even when you thought they were totally absorbed in something else and not paying any attention to your litany of complaints.

"I haven't seen Derek in ages," she replied coldly, swallowing convulsively. Turning to Tom, she said. "Thank-you, Officer. If there's nothing else you need, I'll go now. I want to get back to clean the cottage, and I also must notify my aunt."

"Do you have a phone in the cottage, Miss?"

She gave him an affirmative nod. "But it's not connected, and I won't be staying long enough to make it worthwhile connecting it. I'll have to call Aunt Kate from a pay phone. In fact, I'll do that as soon as I get to a shopping mall. I think you're making too much out of a broken window, but I do appreciate your concern," Jade told him sincerely. It had been a long time since anyone had ever been concerned about her, except for Aunt Kate, of course. But even Aunt Kate maintained a distance. This officer seemed to care, but after her initial gratitude, memories of her Toronto experience pushed to the fore. Jade mentally tossed aside the supposed solicitude of the detective as meaningless lip service.

She left the station quickly, and bypassing the Zeller's store, she drove to Gateway Hardware, hoping it would still be where she remembered it. It was. An old-fashioned hardware store, packed with every conceivable item for Do-it-yourself types, it never failed to captivate her. Dozens of shelves held old-fashioned oil lamps, fittings for pumps, acrylic paints, microwave ovens and laser flashlights. As she was buying the pane of glass--a less complicated matter than she had thought--she chatted with the man behind the counter. He didn't recognize her, but after some explaining by Jade, he finally recalled her aunt and her cousins. He too spoke with a lilting drawl, a combination of his Irish/Scottish ancestors and the *c'est la vie* attitude of the born and bred northerner.

Thanking him for his help, she returned to Zeller's to buy cleaning supplies and toiletries. She also bought a pair of rubber gloves. Her aunt had never used gloves while cleaning or doing dishes and often teased Jade about her fastidiousness. But Jade had refused to fall for the playful insults. Her beautiful hands were proof that the gloves did, indeed, protect her hands, but they also hid the fact that she was a hard worker.

She had no problem finding a pay phone situated just inside the front entrance between the outer and inner sets of doors. As she scrounged in her purse for her aunt's number, she wondered why it had not occurred to her until that moment to contact any of her cousins. Odd. They should have been the first ones she phoned, because they lived closer. One of her cousins lived right in North Bay, while the other girl lived in Restoule. She wasn't sure where Kate's son lived, but presumed that he lived nearby. But maybe she didn't contact them because she knew that they seldom visited the cottage or had anything to do with it. It was almost as if they recognized that the cottage was hers. There was no rancor or envy over Jade's use of the cottage, she knew.

Her cousins were just as generous as her aunt, but there was little in common between Jade and them. Given the circumstances of her upbringing, there couldn't be the shared background that Jade knew existed in many families. She heard Aunt Kate's phone ringing in her Florida condo. *Maybe I just can't sustain a normal relationship with anyone.*

She let the phone ring four times and was just about to hang up when she heard Aunt Kate's beloved voice. Jade felt a calmness sweep over her. She chuckled, as repeatedly her aunt said, "Things would work out much better, if you would just take that damn cottage. Then, you will go there more often. Things like this wouldn't happen."

Jade interrupted to ask about her cousins and found with some surprise that her cousin Rick was living in Toronto. He was the one that Aunt Kate had never understood. Indeed, he was most unlike the rest of Aunt Kate's family. A flash of insight passed through Jade's mind. He's a lot like me, she thought, a lost soul. Yet, why would Rick, the youngest, with a loving mother, a stern but loving father, two doting older sisters be like that? He had been given most things that youngsters wanted, along with the loving guidance that she had lacked in her growing-up years. She wondered what he was doing in Toronto, and promised her aunt to look him up when she returned.

Replacing the telephone receiver, after again reassuring her aunt that everything was fine, she gathered her purchases and returned to her car for the journey back to her bolt hole, unaware that at that very moment, Tom and Jason were discussing the information Jason had found about her.

Something was niggling away in Jason's mind; somewhere in the dark recesses, his mind juggled the pieces, trying to fit the fragments together, but he couldn't quite get them to form a complete picture. It was a gut instinct, the same instinct that had catapulted him to the top of his career at a relatively early age. Sure, he had the education and also the experience, but as far as he was concerned, these were no good without the gut feeling that every good police officer should have. Even with his new-found information, he wanted to protect Jade. God only knew why. She was nothing to him. It was as though Fate were lending a hand, forcing him to take an action he didn't want to take.

"What's up with you, Jay?" Tom had turned to Jason as Jade left the station. Jason explained what he had found out about Jade. Tom's face assumed a bewildered expression and he let out a low whistle. "There must be something more to it, though." He gave Jason a thoughtful look. "Somehow, she doesn't look the type to be involved in trafficking--of any sort," he emphasized. He was acutely aware of the way Jason's mind worked. He also remembered that Jason still hadn't gotten over finding his wife's body in a ditch along Highway 11, a victim of her own carelessness. Like Jade, she had been traveling too quickly to successfully negotiate the curves, and her car had careened off the highway, smashing into a solid wall of granite.

That had been ten years ago. Since then Jay had worked through his rage and guilt by putting in hours of overtime, and his diligence had accelerated his promotions until he was now a detective sergeant in the homicide division in Toronto. He very seldom came north. But at the request of his old friend or to see his Ojibway grandmother with whom he had a unique bond, Jay would drop everything he was doing and come immediately. Tom had met a few of Jason's women friends over the years, but somehow none of the relationships between Jason and a woman ever progressed to a more permanent one.

Tom and Jason had been like brothers, but Tom didn't ask Jay up too often; he knew the memories were still painful, even though the marriage between Jason and his wife had not been all that great. Hell, what marriage was totally great? He frowned as he compared his life to

Jason's. He and Lorraine loved each other and their three kids, and he thought their marriage was as good as any; even so, they had their ups and downs, too, and if anyone were to see the two together in their down period, they would probably figure their marriage was on a short, slippery slope to divorce court.

"We want you to come to dinner tonight," he told Jason, "and we won't take *no* for an answer." Luckily, he and Lorraine were in one of their up periods, so he knew he would have no problem inviting Jason to dinner. "Lorraine is dying to see you and hear all about the big city. I'll call and tell her you're here. She keeps saying that when the kids are grown, she will go to Toronto every other week, just to see some of the shows and get some big-city culture, as she calls it."

Jason grinned. "I accept. Maybe you can talk Lorraine into making her scrumptious wild blueberry pie." It was good to be back in the north. Not that Toronto wasn't great, but the north was part of his culture, the part that couldn't be found in the Toronto that Lorraine longed to absorb. He felt keenly his Ojibway heritage and the enticement of the bush and water. As he contemplated his feelings now, he felt the life source surge through him. He had needed this trip, this return to what he was.

Many Ojibway who had more Native blood than he, didn't particularly like the bush. They were quite content to flow with the times, move into "European" homes, have access to hot showers at the turn of a tap, and watch television while eating micro-waved popcorn. So did he, most of the time. Some First Nations people gave them the derogatory term *Apples*, red on the outside and white on the inside. He didn't see it that way. He often yearned to escape to his heritage in the north country, and when he couldn't make it physically, he would daydream about it or call his grandmother.

His work tied him up in Toronto more often than he

would have liked, yet he had to admit to a feeling of closeness with the city and with his work. He loved the pulsating life that emanated from the hot sidewalks as he walked. He liked looking in the shop windows, smelling the deli essences of bread and spiced meats, the aroma of coffee wafting along the way. He knew that Tom thought it was memory of his dead wife that forced him to stay away from the north, but that was not the whole of it. True, he had felt sorry for both Marty and himself, but even that had lessened over the past few years.

He felt guilty more than anything else, he supposed. It was after one of their quarrels that Marty had gone dashing off late at night in a sports car much like Jade's. Neither of them had been to blame, he thought. It was a case of two people who seemed to rub each other the wrong way whenever they were together. Jason had been aware that Marty had a lot of friends, and nice friends too. He had also had some very good friends, still did. So somebody must have liked them, he thought. It was just that together the friction between them overcame everything else--even the great sex they had between them.

When he thought of sex, an image of Jade superimposed itself over Marty's face. There was a similarity between her and Marty but, even knowing as little as he did about Jade, he felt the superficiality of that likeness. It hadn't been a physical resemblance. Jade's eyes were green, her long white-blond hair hung loosely and straight down her back. She was beautiful, he supposed, if you liked tall girls with long legs and small breasts. He wasn't particularly partial to them himself. Marty had been petite and dark, with short-cropped black hair and blue eyes, his kind of woman.

No, it wasn't a physical likeness to his dead wife that Jade possessed. It had to be some inner quality. Jade, however, struck him as being more mature, more in control of all that life threw her way. To say that he had been shocked when he had unearthed the information about her when he had talked to Toronto headquarters was an understatement. Jade didn't look like a person who could be used as a patsy. She looked quite capable of standing up for herself. So just how much did she know about this Derek's involvement with the cocaine trade? Then he asked himself the question he had been asking ever since the previous night: Why was he so interested in her? What did he care what she had done or hadn't done?

Jason snapped sharply out of his inner analysis just in time to hear Tom explaining his curiosity over the window in Jade's cottage. There had been a homicide in the area a few months before, and Tom wondered if there was any connection. They hadn't even thought of the cottage at the time. Or maybe they had, but there had been nothing to connect the homicide with it. The victim had been a young girl of 23, whose description was similar to Jade's. This is what had triggered Tom's suspicions. Her throat had been slit, but not before she had been viciously raped. Tom had wanted Jay to lend his expertise to the case, even before Jade had walked into the building that morning, but now it seemed doubly imperative that he do so. The girl had been from out of the province, apparently hitchhiking to Oshawa, Ontario to see a sister. Her murderer had not been found; nor had the police found any motive for the killing. This was what worried Tom, and he related his fears to Jason.

Oblivious to any gnawing concerns her story had aroused in the two police officers, Jade traveled back over her route to the cottage. The hot July weather had brought out all the wild flowers along the route. Just past Cedar Heights Road, the highway wove through a montage of white daisies, twinkling their yellow powder-puff eyes at the orange and yellow Devil's paint brushes. Here and there, wild yellow snapdragons put forth their cheery display, and always in the background was the dusty green northern bush.

As she drew closer to the cottage, small lakes and bays appeared, calm and glistening in the noon sunlight, unaware that even now, cranberry bogs were threatening to overtake small ponds and inlets in nature's evolutionary ecosystem. When Jade drove into the rutted dirt path that passed for a driveway, she was bewildered by the presence of the unmarked car from the previous night. In it was the detective from Toronto. *Oh God! Am I never going to be free from my past?* Was it going to haunt her even up here in the north? True, Marten River was not all that far from Toronto, a mere 390 kilometers, but it was far enough for Jade to have expected some degree of seclusion. She didn't have anything to do with cocaine--not then, not now--but no one was ready to believe that, least of all, it seemed, some macho cop from the big city. All this passed through Jade's mind as she maneuvered her small car to the front of the cottage.

To her right was the glade that she so loved. Small and basin shaped, it was now overgrown with long grass, ferns and wild flowers, but for the most part the underbrush that she and Kate had spent the summer four years past cutting out had not grown back with its usual rampant growth. Odd, that. Usually it came back very quickly, sometimes within a week.

The midday sun was now overhead and shone into the glade through the maples and birch trees. At the back of the glade flowed the stream, shallow at this particular spot but deeper farther into the bush. It skipped along now, talking to her as it always had in the past. In her mind, she often created voices from the babbling waters. Or maybe they *were* voices, and she had somehow tuned in to them. Often, the edges between reality and her visions and powers became blurred.

She had known since childhood that she had an uncanny

intuition, a seemingly haunting quality that often unnerved those with whom she associated. Why, if her powers were supposedly so great, didn't her intuition keep her out of the scrapes and messes into which she was always getting herself? Like now.

Forcing her mind to the moment, she surveyed the familiar ground before her. She would have to scythe the weeds down in the glade before she could ever get the lawnmower over it, she grimaced. A good place for snakes to hide. She loathed snakes. She hoped there would be none in the overgrown basin. Regular grass cutting she didn't mind. One of Aunt Kate's quirks was that although this was a cottage and visited very seldom, she felt that it should have the best equipment available. "Just because it's a cottage," Aunt Kate had argued with Jade one summer, "it needn't be the repository for all the garbage that's not wanted anywhere else. Besides, where else do you need good tools but in the very place you're going to use them the most?"

She blessed Kate for this now, as she realized the work that she had before her to get the cottage into shape. When she had telephoned her aunt, she had adamantly refused to phone one of her cousins to help when Kate had worriedly suggested the possibility. She had not told Kate all about the latest episode in Toronto. Kate knew only the little information that Jade had felt obligated to tell her about her relationship with Derek.

Jade hadn't told her about how she, too, had been questioned. She knew her aunt would fly back from Florida and cluck around her like a mother hen. This she could do without. Kate tried very hard not to be the clucking hen type, knowing that Jade, not being used to having a doting mother around, abhorred the idea, but somehow, things always worked out that this is what happened. Probably why Aunt Kate stayed longer and longer in Florida each year, Jade chuckled to herself, smiling fondly at her mental picture of her aunt. She wouldn't want to fuss around her own children, either.

Jason was already leaning against the exterior of his car, but he did not attempt to come over to hers until she extricated herself gracefully from the low-slung vehicle. He didn't understand why or how, but for some odd reason, he knew that Jade needed a few minutes to adjust to his being there. As she swung her body out, she stared at his tall, lithe frame. There was an aura about him that reminded her of Derek. She couldn't quite put her finger on it, but it was there--something in the way he walked, the authority that he exuded; but as Jade knew, that air of authority didn't mean much. After all, Derek had it and look at what he was really like. He had been caught trafficking in all kinds of illicit drugs.

She mentally compared the two men as she made her way slowly over to him. Where Derek's eyes had been gray, this man's were midnight black. Where Derek's hair had been wavy blond, this man's was black and straight--what there was left after his military style haircut. Yet there was that indefinable something that connected the two men.

"What are you doing here?" she snapped waspishly at him. She couldn't help it; her experience with police officers had been all bad. She still choked up every time the memories insinuated their way into her thoughts.

"I would like to look over the place, if you don't mind." His voice was calm, more so when he recognized her mood.

"Would it matter if I did mind?" she asked him bluntly. "I'm sure that if you have decided to look the place over, then you will, if you haven't already."

"No." He chose to ignore the roundabout query. Intuitively, he knew that her experiences so far had not been all that positive. He gave her a calculating scrutiny. She appeared quite capable of looking after herself, and as her driver's licence had placed her at 26, she would probably be one of those liberated females who wanted to be in control at all times. *She isn't the type to cling to you,* a small voice echoed through his mind. He mentally shrugged it away.

"I would just like to familiarize myself with the surroundings." He put up a hand to forestall any outburst. "And before you come out with another nasty comment, I have looked at some of the other cottages in this area. So, no, I am not just zeroing in on you, whatever you may think."

Suddenly weary of the whole situation, and beyond caring about cops, drugs, or anything to do with her past life, she told him to go ahead. She wanted to get on with her work, needed the challenge of physical labor to quiet her jangled nerves. Innate good manners, however, did come to the fore long enough for her to offer to make coffee. He took her up on her offer and headed off in the direction of the glade. Jade turned the key in the lock.

Everything was just as messy as she had left it that morning. "No fairy godmother here to put things back into shape," she muttered grimly. She was glad that she had turned on the switch for the hot water heater the night before. It had taken some time to prime the pump after its being out of commission for so long, but eventually she had coaxed it into doing its job. She had drained the cold water tank once already just to make sure that the water she would use for coffee and cooking would be fresh.

Stepping into the cottage now, she made her way to the sink and the cupboards. The cottage had one room that did for both kitchen and living room, with a small counter separating the two areas. It was all in pine logs--beautiful to Aunt Kate and many other people, but it really did not satisfy Jade's aesthetic taste. The cupboards, which Jade did like, lent a startling burnt orange contrast to the pine logs. As she stepped over the debris on the floor, she stopped short, her eyes moving to the broken window. Her heart heaved up into her throat, and she gasped in fright.

"What's wrong?" A quiet voice behind her sent an after-shock rippling through her already vulnerable system. She jumped and gasped, as Jason's comforting hand descended on her shoulder; she knew he could feel her trembling.

"When I left this morning, I left that cupboard pulled across that window. It's quite heavy and clumsy to move. That's what I did last night when I found the window broken."

He looked where she pointed. The top part of the cupboard now covered only half the window, having been slid along the enamel top of the antique base for half its length. The small shards of glass that remained in the window were minimal. Enough room, he conjectured, for a person to climb through. "Stay here," he ordered, not questioning her assertion for a moment.

He had no gun that she could see, but he quickly looked about the room, then looked into the bedroom that she had occupied the previous night. He found nothing under the queen size bed or in the closet. Yet his cop's instinct told him that somebody had been there.

He was momentarily disconcerted as his glance slid to Jade's short nightshirt, a pink oversized T-shirt with a picture of a brown teddy bear on the front being held in a pair of masculine arms. It had been tossed carelessly across the bed, and for the first time in many months, he felt his groin muscles tighten and his pants bulged. He was embarrassed and glad he had told her to stay in the other room. He was reacting just like some horny kid whose testosterone levels were kicking in with a vengeance.

He forced himself to look at the bedroom window. Nothing wrong there that he could see. There was a strong screen over the window, and over that, iron security bars. This aunt of hers sure knew what she was doing, he applauded mentally. He went into the small bathroom and looked at the window there--no bars, only a light screen--and the opening too small for anyone but a child to get through. In the other small bedroom, there was unused furniture strewn everywhere. But even here there were bars across the window. Returning to the front door, he noticed that there was a thick two-by-four that could be dropped down over the door and slid into an iron U-shaped hook for protection at night, or any other time, he mentally added. The only vulnerable part of the cottage that he could make out was the one window in the living room/kitchen that lacked protection. He analyzed it now.

"When did your aunt put the security bars across the windows?" he asked, more comfortable now that he had his muscles and hormones under firm, disciplined control.

"About ten years ago, when she decided that she would no longer be visiting the cottage as much, and she made it available to me." She was hugging herself for comfort. He found himself wanting to put his arms around her to give her his strength. He held back, not wanting to probe too deeply into his feelings. "It's typical of Aunt Kate to think of all this." Jade was saying. "But I'm sure there was a security bar over this window too. It seems odd to put them on all the large windows except this one, doesn't it?" She turned to Jason with a querying look that said more than any words, *Please, please tell me everything is all right.*

He was leaning against the pine log wall, looking quite casual and virile in his tan corduroys and yellow polo shirt. Years of practice dictated that he not lie to her, even though he wanted to, even though he longed to assuage her fears. "Hm, yes." He didn't want to give too much away, but he was concerned. After his conference with Tom, his gut feeling was that nothing was as it seemed here. He wasn't even sure of Jade. Hell, he thought, he wasn't even sure of himself anymore. If anyone had mentioned yesterday that some girl, running scared from Toronto, would turn him on, he would have laughed uproariously in the person's face. The last thing he needed was to get involved with a liberated woman who was also involved in drugs, he chided himself.

"Probably some kids in the neighborhood," he told Jade now, hoping what he said not only had the ring of truth, but was the truth. "They might have noticed the place was always deserted and decided to look it over." He wasn't at all sure that it was *some kids*, but he didn't want to frighten her either. And she *was* frightened. Although she tried desperately to cover it up, her fear jumped out at him like a deer's when it is caught in the glare of headlights.

"How would you like me to put the pane of glass back in for you?" he asked. "You did get one, didn't you?" He tried to sound nonchalant and unconcerned.

"Yes, it's in the car, along with a package of putty."

Her voice sounded calmer to him and he didn't want to do or say anything that might raise either fear or anger in her. He hoped secretly that he wouldn't have to cut the pane. For one thing, that would mean either going back into town to look for a glass cutter or going fourteen kilometers to Tom's house at Tomiko Lake. This would mean a delay regardless of where he went. He didn't want to leave Jade any longer than he had to. Besides, he admitted silently, he really wasn't all that good as a handyman and cringed at the thought of trying to cut the pane of glass. He was sure she wouldn't have a glass cutter. Probably she had bought a large pane of glass, thinking it was a better bargain. Isn't that what women did? After all, if she had left the cupboard across the window as she said she had, she obviously hadn't measured properly for the new glass.

When he came back with the glass and the putty, she commented, "There's a glass cutter in the shed if you need it, but I don't think you will; I measured the window pretty accurately I think."

He was brought up short. So much for his chauvinistic thinking. "When did you measure it?"

"This morning. That's how I know I left the cupboard across the window; I went outside and measured from that side. It's only four feet from the ground."

He hated to give her credit for being efficient. His male ego brought down a notch, he reluctantly managed to get out a mumbled acknowledgment that she couldn't quite hear. She smiled as she recognized his masculine reluctance to credit women with having any common sense. Men! They would compliment a woman on her hair, on her looks, on her cooking, even on how good she was in bed, but at the mention of common sense, they felt they owned it all.

"Thank you," she smiled sweetly, even though she couldn't be sure that what he had just said was a compliment.

As he set out to repair the window, she started to vacuum all the dust that had settled and all the animal droppings that she had been too tired to clean up the night before. Noticing him struggling with the heavy two-piece Dutch cupboard, she moved quickly to help him. It seemed much heavier than it had the previous night, but that could have been a case of necessity giving her the extra strength she had needed. He mentioned the weight of it now.

"Aunt Kate keeps all her kettles and pots for the outdoor barbecue in the bottom cupboard and various other paraphernalia in the metal drawers. This cupboard is over a hundred years old. I believe Aunt Kate inherited it from a relative; she didn't want it in her house and she didn't want to give it up, so she brought it up to the cottage as a sort of compromise. I pulled only the top half over last night, because I couldn't move the whole cupboard, but even so, it seems heavier than it did then." She gave him a wry smile.

The soothing gurgle of the coffee trickling through the

filter diverted her thoughts. Always when she was upset, the fragrance and aroma of fresh coffee managed to comfort her. She quickly vacuumed up the dirt from the pine floors of the living room/kitchen, then decided to give everything a rinse with water and disinfectant before tackling the bedroom and bathroom. Jason, having found a pair of heavy gloves in his car, worked on the window, carefully removing any small shards of glass that remained in the undamaged frame.

The hominess wasn't lost upon either of them. Jade offered him coffee, startling herself by the way she accepted his being there, liking the comforting feeling his presence gave her. "Why do you come up here?" she asked him as she poured his coffee. "I wouldn't expect a city person to like this place."

"I used to live here," he told her with pride. "I live most of the time in Toronto, but at one time I was one of many Ojibway natives in this area."

She looked at him. "Native?" she queried, and noticed his face take on a defensive mask. She hadn't meant to offend him. It was just that he barely looked native--maybe his dark eyes--but that was all.

He gazed at her, expecting a rebuff. Well she could just go to hell. He would drink his coffee and leave. He felt he had earned that much at least. Even now, it was a sore point with him that many people had stereotyped him as a lazy slob simply because he had Ojibway blood in him.

"I'm part Ojibway." His defensiveness held pride. "My father was Scottish and my mother was Ojibway from Bear Island."

Her only comment was: "That's what accounts for your dark obsidian eyes, I guess. Are your parents still living?" Where was her white European snobbishness? She didn't sound as though she felt superior to him, just curious.

"No, they both died together several years ago. In a car accident. Both had been drinking," he told her bitterly.

"That's why I don't drink very much myself. My Ojibway grandmother raised me to have enough moral strength not to have to rely on alcohol."

Jade looked at him with understanding. "I don't drink very much, either," she said. "Although sometimes I wish I did. I'm sure it would help temporarily."

"Two weird people," he muttered. "Maybe we should team up together." The minute he said it, although it had been jokingly uttered, he felt that it would be the right thing to do--and also very wrong. For one thing, they knew nothing about each other, and for another, she had been involved with a drug dealer. He felt his hope slipping quietly into the background. His life would go on as it had.

He had finished the window, noticing as he did so that at one time there had been security bars across it, just as she had said. He said nothing to Jade, hesitating to frighten her more than she already was. The large front windows had double shutters on both the outside and the inside, so that when a person left the cottage, both sets could be locked up. On the inside, there was a large bar that could be lowered across the shutters, similar to the one on the door. As Jade had noted earlier, this window seemed to be the only vulnerable spot in the cottage.

CHAPTER THREE

He knew he should be going, but he couldn't pull himself away. "I'm on a sort of holiday myself. Why don't I help you get the yard cleaned up? No strings attached," he added quickly, just in case she got the wrong idea. Jade was about to refuse; he could see it in her eyes and in the way she was composing her features, preparing to say *no* as politely as she could.

"Thank-you," Jade surprised herself. "If you like, you could start in the glade. That's my favorite spot, but I really don't like going into it when the grass is long. I bought some blackfly repellent today while I was out. You may use it, and, for when it doesn't work, and it usually doesn't, there's an After-Bite pen you daub on before you scratch," she laughed. "I don't know about you, but blackflies and mosquitoes consider me their most delicious part of their meal. I swell up for days afterward, even though I've been coming here for years."

"I wish you hadn't reminded me." He let out a soft groan. "I swell up too, and some of my ancestors lived in this bush a thousand years ago. You would think by now I would be immune to the damn things." He scratched his arm in an unconscious anticipation of an itch.

They both burst out laughing. It was the first time in weeks that Jade had felt light hearted. Already, this place was working its magic on her. Somehow, though, she rather imagined that her unusual and rare elation had something to do with the dark, virile cop before her. Both stopped laughing at the same time and looked at each other in wonderment. Jason was the first to turn away.

"I'd better find a scythe." His voice was hoarse with desire. "And also the fly dope." Even the blackflies and mosquitoes, he reasoned, were better than standing here feeling like some adolescent kid infatuated for the first time. He was thirty-six, too old for her anyway. She probably looked on him as an uncle, if not a father figure, when she wasn't looking at him as a chauvinist cop. It surprised him how well he could assess what she was thinking. He knew she was frightened, but he would swear that she wasn't frightened of him. He figured *wary* would be a more accurate term.

He scythed the grass quickly, then raked it up and put it in the compost heap he had discovered beside the brown metal shed. In the shed, he found the lawnmower, and examined it closely to see if it was in running order. It was a good one, he noted, that mulched as it cut. Suddenly he frowned. Jade had remarked about the scarcity of undergrowth in the glade, adding that she and her aunt had last cut it about four years ago. In this area, the lack of underbrush would have been nothing short of a miracle. Now he thought he knew why the glade was relatively clear.

The mower had definitely been used for heavy cutting, but more than that, it had traces of recent gasoline in it, and Jason was sure that neither Jade nor her aunt would have left gasoline in the mower when they stored it. Even if they had, it would have evaporated long ago and left a sticky residue. Pieces of a puzzle were beginning to fall into place, but he had no idea of what the whole represented.

Inside the cottage, Jade thoroughly scoured the living/kitchen area and cleaned the wood-burning fireplace. She poured herself a second cup of coffee. She had tackled her bedroom first, getting rid of the dust, then going over everything with a cloth dipped in Lysol disinfectant. That was one thing she and her aunt had in common, she reflected. They were both clean freaks. Jade always felt that the cleanliness helped to clear her mind, and left her time to work on her writing assignments.

She had often heard just the opposite, that a cluttered home meant an uncluttered brain. It was like projecting all the mind's clutter onto the exterior world. Jade thought now that the two opposite opinions would never be resolved, and although she was beginning to think that the other point of view may be right, she continued to clean the cottage in her usual energetic way. The newly remade bed raised her spirits when she smoothed her favorite pale yellow comforter over it. Against the pine it looked fresh and vibrant, and she was pleased with the uplifting effect. Nevertheless, try as she might, she could not rid herself of a deep-seated unease and a feeling that she was not alone in the cottage. She chastised herself. Of course she wasn't alone. That cop was outside, supposedly helping her, but probably using that as an excuse to snoop around.

She proceeded to scour the bathroom. It was much dirtier than she had ever noticed before . . . almost as if someone had been using it. There were dark hairs on the floor and inside the tub and soap splashes on the beige tiles on the floor. Unsettling thoughts stabbed at her, begging for attention, but she couldn't afford to let her mind wander in that direction. She was too fragile, desperately in need of keeping her mind clear. Her cousins must be using the cottage more than she had thought.

Disgusted with the sloppy habits of her cousins, she vigorously scrubbed at the mess, then decided to give the small bedroom, used for storage, only a cursory dusting and vacuuming. She could always keep the door closed if the clutter bothered her too much. Reaching into the corner for the vacuum cleaner, she noticed Jason talking to a man who had turned into the driveway in a black Ford Fiesta. The man was smiling, and from Jade's vantage point at the window, seemed to be asking for directions. Jason came to the door as she retreated to the small bedroom.

"There's someone here looking for a Rick Beamer," he called to her.

"That's my cousin," she yelled back over the whine of the vacuum. "He lives in Toronto, or so my aunt says. I don't think he ever comes up here." She wondered fleetingly who would be looking for Rick in this area.

Jason pulled back and closed the door. She looked beautiful. Her energetic cleaning frenzy had brought more color to her features, and dust smudges on her cheeks added to her appeal. He shook himself and returned to the car. The man looked at him warily. Something about him aroused Jason's suspicions, but there was nothing specific about the man or his behavior that he could pinpoint.

Thanking him with a guarded look in his eyes and distrust in his voice, the man backed the car slowly out the driveway. Because of the trees, Jason could not see which direction the man took, but through years of training and discipline, he had consigned the licence plate and descriptions of the man and the car to his memory. He had told Jade he would finish the cutting, so he decided to get that out of the way first. He wanted Jade to move out of the cottage, but recognized the futility of that idea. They may have established a tentative rapport, but he didn't think her trust would extend to heeding his request to move out, especially as she had nowhere else to go--and certainly wouldn't leave just because he asked her to.

In the small, cluttered room, Jade reached down to retrieve an obstruction from the greedy maw of the vacuum. She gasped. There, entwined tenaciously in the bristles of the floor sweeper, was a polyethylene bag of white powder. She noticed several more packages of a white substance stashed under the bed amid boxes and cartons of unused items. Having been with Derek, she recognized it immediately as cocaine. In another box were packages of marijuana. Appalled at the incriminating evidence before her, she bolted upright, her mind a jumble of incoherent thoughts. Suddenly she felt a sickening pain as something heavy smashed into the back of her head. Just before blackness enveloped her, she thought she screamed for Jason, but whether any sound actually came out, she didn't know.

***

The day was sparkling. After the rain of the previous night, the poplar leaves, the mauve fireweed, yellow jewelweed, lilac milkweed, the black-eyed susans, all danced and flaunted their resplendent jewels. It was the type of day Jade loved. The air was still, waiting for the hot sun to slake its thirst from the dew-spattered plants. She drove on, searching, searching; it seemed all her life she had been searching. Suddenly her head pivoted. There to her right, just visible through the poplar and maple trees, was a picturesque clearing. In the background, she could see a quietly flowing stream. It was a perfect place--the one for which she had been looking all her life. Without hesitation she drove into the smooth asphalt driveway, feeling comfortable being there. It was unusual to find a paved driveway in this part of tourist country, she mused, intending to comment on it if she found anyone at home.

The driveway was shaded, but Jade didn't find it in the least depressing. Nothing could be dispiriting with that beautiful sunlit vista at the end of the driveway. Birds chirruped in the trees. She recognized the ubiquitous robin, the raucous voice of the blue jay, and somewhere, faintly, she could hear the grosbeaks and the American finches. Her heart filled with joy. In the distance, she heard the laugh of the loon, and suddenly stopped. Today it was a laugh; at other times the loon could sound maniacally sad. She had once asked a university friend whether he found the loon's call happy or melancholy, and was surprised to learn that most people thought it happy. She had always found it cheerless and haunting. But today the series of calls seemed to bear out the others' views.

She broke through the dappled shade of the driveway into the clearing and gasped with disbelief; a thrill of enchantment twinkled through her.

The cottage was beautiful--out of a fairy tale. It seemed to be an anomaly in this part of the country, more in keeping with the English cottages of her dreams. Yet here it was, in this glade, white stucco, low and rambling, as she had always imagined. Yet she knew that it had been built with the cold northern winters in mind. She didn't know how she knew, but she did. An elderly woman appeared in the open doorway. Something about her was familiar, but Jade could not place the stranger at that moment. The woman smiled at her in recognition. Intuiting the woman's longing to talk to someone, Jade heeded the unspoken request for company.

Getting out of her car, she smiled in return and started to apologize for her intrusion into this paradise. The woman still smiled and shook her white head, brushing off Jade's apology. Feeling a tremor of shock, Jade knew that the woman had been expecting her. How? Who was she? After a brief examination of her feelings, she discovered she was more perplexed than frightened.

"I couldn't help coming in here," Jade told the woman. "Your place is beautiful. It's a place I've always dreamed of."

The woman, who looked to be in her eighties, gave her a beautiful smile and nodded. Jade followed the woman about the yard admiring all the flowers in the gardens, looking at the fern-bordered forest with the whispering stream edging the back of the garden. She remarked on the lupines in their colors of pink and purple; she gloried in the sweet-smelling yellow lilies. The wild red poppies near the edge of the clearing sent a thrill of anticipation through her.

Throughout the garden tour, the woman was serene. Smiling at Jade with recognition and love, the elderly woman silently beckoned her into the cottage. Jade surmised that the woman, although longing for her company, could not talk to her but seemed to understand each word that Jade had spoken. Jade nodded enthusiastically. She knew what the cottage would be like, every single detail.

With anticipation, she stepped into the sunlit interior. The living room overlooked the glade and the stream, yet the trees didn't cast dark, threatening shadows into the surroundings. The room was bright from the sunlight streaming in through the well-insulated skylight and through the large energy-efficient picture window. The kitchen and dining areas were a hostess's dream. The morning sun poured in, uplifting everything in the room.

Just outside the kitchen door was a herb garden, walled and partially covered with lattice. One could go through the kitchen door into the garden and not have to worry about meeting up with anything other than the hundreds of birds that perched and darted and dipped about the yard. In the same area was a small kitchen garden. She recognized carrots, beets, peppers, tomatoes--her favorites. The remainder of the yard was grass, with a few apple trees and two small pear trees planted strategically at the edge of the lawn. Jade had never felt so completely at peace.

The woman didn't offer to show her the rest of the cottage. Nevertheless, Jade knew that it contained three bedrooms and a den besides the rooms she had seen. The woman busied herself with plugging in the kettle and putting out two cups and saucers for tea--Earl Grey, Jade noted. It was that kind of morning, she thought--a splendid, relaxing, let-the-world-wait morning.

As she anticipated her tea, Jade glanced about the room. In the dining area was a set of pictures. Some looked to be recent, a few from long ago. The woman looked over and caught Jade's glance as Jade picked up the more recent picture showing a loving couple. The woman she recognized as the one before her. The man looked older still, but serene and happy. A flash of recognition passed through her, and along with it a sudden chill as she gazed at an older version of Jason. The woman's face turned sad, and Jade knew that the man had died. As the woman lovingly touched her arm, Jade glanced at the date scrawled in a shaky hand on the photo; she couldn't make out the first two numerals, but the last two were "46." She looked at the pictures of three handsome children, two girls and one boy, pictures of various babies of all ages in all poses, well loved and cherished.

"How old was your husband?" Jade whispered as a cold hand seemed to clutch her. But the woman either did not hear her or could not answer. Jade drank her tea in companionable silence until she felt herself slipping away, not quite knowing what was happening. She wondered briefly if the woman had put some sort of drug in her tea. A hammer was pounding her brain and her vision blurred, sharpened for a second, then blurred again. She squeezed her eyes tightly shut, then with sheer will power, forced them to open.

***

Through a mind-numbing fog, she realized she was in a strange bed with two worried police officers bending over her. The cop from Toronto looked positively ill, she noted. Tom, the guy from the North Bay station, had noticed her regaining consciousness. "The doctor will be here shortly."

She was still confused and hovering between two worlds. Half of her was still in the cottage of her dream, part of her was here. Wherever *here* was. She didn't know which was reality--or if either was.

"I found my cottage," she murmured huskily. Both men

looked uncomfortable and distressed. Her mouth was dry and her tongue refused to work properly, causing her words to sound slurred.

"God, Jade," Jason's voice was harsh. "You could have been killed."

"I found something that looked like cocaine," Jade mumbled, gradually coming back to the present–"and possibly marijuana. How did they get there? Oh, my God, you--you think I put it there, don't you? Or that I knew it was there? Do you think I put it there last night?" She pressed him, suddenly anxious to hear his reply.

"It wasn't last night," he said thickly, ignoring her question for the moment. "You've been out for two days. We didn't know what was going to happen to you."

"Two days?" She croaked. "Was that long enough to get to my cottage?" Jason didn't know what she was talking about, but then again, she realized, neither did she. The date "46" popped into her mind. But she tried to ignore it. Between her visions and her weird relationships, no wonder she needed therapy.

Jason, oblivious to her inner turmoil, was more concerned about what was going on in the *now*. He and Tom, going on instinct, had gone over all the characteristics of the homicide that Tom had called Jason to the area to investigate, and Jade's supposed involvement with drugs in Toronto. Tom had been adamant that Jade's involvement was peripheral at most. Jason wasn't so sure. Still, a crucial element was missing.

"Jade, you were hit over the head with an iron," Jason anguished. "The guy must have been hiding in the bottom of that two-piece cupboard. Neither of us thought to open up the bottom door. No wonder we thought it was heavy; that was the only place I didn't look." He was upset. "I can't believe I didn't open it to check." He repeatedly slapped his fist into his open hand, causing a slap, slap, slap noise that echoed in Jade's head. It must have jarred

Tom, too, because when he spoke up, he sounded irritable.

"Jason, calm down." Tom touched his arm. "The guy would have had to scrunch himself up into a ball to get into that cupboard. Anybody could have missed him."

"Do you mean he was there when we got back from town?" Jade gulped, horrified, as the significance sunk into her befuddled mind. To think that someone had been there, listening to their conversation, and they hadn't even known it! She felt vulnerable and shaky.

"We got the cocaine and the marijuana," Jason told her. "But we didn't get the guy. I thought I heard you scream and looked up from scything the grass just in time to catch a glimpse of the man running out the driveway." He didn't want to tell her that he'd had his doubts about the man in the Ford Fiesta, but then had shrugged off his suspicions. Evidently, there were at least two men involved with the drugs. He was slipping, he castigated himself. His mind, instead of being on his work, had been on Jade, now lying in a bed in Tom's house, looking young and vulnerable.

"Out, you guys," Tom's wife appeared in the doorway with a man Jade assumed to be the doctor. "Out, out! Hi!" she said to Jade cheerfully. "Not the best way to meet, but I'm Lorraine, Tom's wife. I'll talk to you when you're feeling better. This is Dr. Shenko. Gruff, but lovable."

The man gave Lorraine a non-committal glance and nodded to Jade, who felt immediately comfortable with him. "How do you feel?" he asked Jade with compassion.

"A little bewildered, a little sore, somewhat confused," she answered him.

"That's to be expected. You had one heck of a bang on your head. You've got a concussion and I had to put seven stitches in your scalp. You should have been taken to hospital, but Jay and Tom wouldn't hear of it. However, I'm not questioning the judgement of these guys." His tone and look belied his words. Jade was sure he was doing just that, or had done that when she had first been hurt. "I'm merely here to see that you're feeling better."

"I felt better when I was out," Jade told him, with a wry smile. "I had an intriguing visit with an old lady at her cottage. And my head wasn't pounding."

"Hmm." He looked at her sharply. "Vivid dreams sometimes occur. The mind is a funny thing, and we don't really understand it at all. Often in cases like this, it seems to drag up fragments from the past, worries that we have, and put them all together in a fashion that would create several novels."

She laughed. "I am a writer. Well, not a well-known one, but I have written three or four articles for magazines."

"Really?" He looked interested. "Well, I don't think you have to worry about your dream. You'll be fine. You're young and strong. A day or two in bed here, and then come to see me in my office . . . just to make sure. The stitches will have to stay in for about a week."

She nodded. She didn't want to stay here in this strange house, even if Tom's wife did seem to be a charming and lovable person. She didn't want to go back to her aunt's cottage either, but she couldn't tell them that. Dare she go back to Toronto? Again, she felt confused and adrift, while life flitted by all around her. She didn't fit in. She wanted to black out again and find the cottage of her dream. She had felt comfortable there; she knew that was where she belonged. There was only one problem--she didn't know how to get there or where it was. She certainly couldn't ask someone. That would land her in a psychiatric ward for sure. Right then and there she decided that the best thing to do would be to gird up her loins and return to Aunt Kate's cottage. Even if she was frightened, she decided, at least she knew the place. Dr. Shenko left with a cheery wave. She explained her decision to an astonished Tom and Jason when they returned to her room.

"You can't go back there, Jade." Tom remonstrated with

her, looking to Jason for support. "You're not safe. We didn't want to tell you, but there was a homicide in that area a few months ago. That's why Jason is here. I wanted his help. The other day when I questioned you? I could see you thought I was overdoing it, but the murdered girl looked something like you. That's why I interrogated you so thoroughly."

Jason had been standing thoughtfully at the window, his taut body at odds with his incongruous apparel. He was clad in jeans and a white T-shirt with pictures of Seagram's Coolers in shades of berry and green. He looked tired and overwrought. Tom looked almost as he had when she had first seen him--a laid-back, happily married man, but now his face was creased with a concerned frown. She had the feeling that he would be more at ease with her out of his house, however much he might protest to the contrary. He had three young teenagers whom she could now hear running noisily about the house as his wife tried unsuccessfully to hush them. Suddenly Jade giggled and Jason gave her a startled look.

"What's so funny?" The question burst from both men at the same time, telling Jade how tense they really were.

"Nothing," Jade chortled. "It's just that you two look nothing like the stereotype of police officers." Tom and Jason both looked at her in chagrin.

"You're staying here." The command was a unified effort.

"I'm leaving," Jade announced firmly. "Maybe I'll even go back to Toronto. But first, I'm going back to the cottage. I have to."

Tom would have argued more, but Jason just gave her an exasperated look and nodded. "Okay," he said, resignedly. "I'll drive you back."

Tom's wife was feeling half affronted and half glad, Jade noticed. But Jade explained that she felt she had to return to the cottage: "It's very good of you to try to keep the children quiet. I know how hard that is," Jade continued, mentally making a note to repay the woman's kindness somehow.

She and Jason drove back to the cottage in silence. When they were nearly there, Jason remarked: "I looked in on the cottage this morning and searched it thoroughly, so it should be safe." When they drew up in the driveway, Jade immediately thought of the cottage of her dreams. It was in an area somewhat like this one, she thought. But not quite. There had been a subtle difference in the surroundings--apart from the fact that the garden of her dream had been well tended, and the cottages were poles apart in the way they were constructed

She noticed a police car pulled up just outside the cottage, with a bored-looking young officer sitting in it. Jason helped Jade out of his car and then went over to the constable. Jade waited for him, leaning against his car, the same one he had used the night he had stopped her for speeding. She allowed herself to wonder at the turn of events. Were there such things as coincidences or fate? Jason turned towards Jade, his relieved expression erasing the worry lines that had been in his face for the last two days.

"There will be somebody watching the place at all times for the next little while." He wanted to ask her about this Rick fellow. He must have been the one in the cupboard, the one the man in the black Fiesta was looking for. But now was not the time to ask her any questions about her cousin. She still looked tired from her ordeal and not a little frightened, but was trying hard to maintain control. He noted that she always had herself under control, and mentioned this to her now.

He didn't know, she thought as she looked at him warily, that she'd had years to perfect the ability. The one time she had let herself be even the least little bit out of control she had ended up with Derek, and look where that had landed her!

Jason helped her into the cottage, as she was still unsteady on her feet. He supported her with one arm and used the other hand to turn the key in the lock. As she leaned on him, a sense of trust and completeness enveloped her.

Jason felt his jeans tighten across his thighs. He became horny at the most inopportune moments, he decided. Hoping Jade wouldn't notice, he went on to explain about the officer who was guarding the cottage. He willed his body to relax and thought he was doing a pretty good job.

Jade had noticed the bulging jeans too, but looked away. My God, the cop could be aroused at the most awkward times, she thought with amazement, unaware of the vulnerable and sexy image that she projected. Even as the flippant thought passed through her mind, she felt for the first time in months her stomach muscles tighten, and noticed that her breasts had become rigid beneath the light T-shirt she was wearing. She had felt somewhat embarrassed when Jason had brought a complete change of clothes for her when he arrived that morning. She wasn't used to having men go through her suitcase and through her underwear. But later, she was glad. She had felt much better after her shower and the change of clothes. Now, however, the tiredness was beginning to overtake her again. When he finally released the lock and they entered the cottage, she offered to make coffee and a sandwich for both of them.

He shook his head. "I'll make the coffee and something for both of us. You sit and relax."

She did as he ordered, not having the strength to take umbrage at his high-handed tone. The comfortable armchair by the window cradled her as the midday sun caressed her aching body. But the physical movement of the car ride and the short walk had started up the pounding in her head. Images of the dream cottage came back, along with snippets of conversation. Bits and pieces of her dream jelled into one confused picture, slipping off to the side, just out of focus.

Jason filled the automatic coffee maker and flipped the switch. He turned, noticed her discomfort, and came over to her. "The doctor said it would take some time to get over the concussion and shock." Jade didn't seem to hear, but felt compelled to tell him about her problem.

"I keep having this vision," she murmured lethargically, leaning back into the soft chair. She didn't go into detail, but deep down in her soul she felt she could tell him everything and he would understand.

"Do you want a pill for your headache?"

She nodded gingerly through the excruciating pain. Jason left and returned a moment later with a glass of water and two capsules from the bottle the doctor had given her. As she gulped the capsules, he put his warm hands on her head and cradled her against him. The pounding stopped even before the capsules could take effect.

"You're better than any medicine," she told him through a befuddled haze.

He smiled. He wanted to hold her. He wanted to love her. The thought shocked him. *What am I doing?* There was still this business of narcotics charges in Toronto, and cocaine and marijuana in the cottage. He felt sure that she wasn't on anything herself. She had told him that she knew nothing about the cocaine or any other drugs, and he believed her, but there was still something which made him wary. He started to withdraw, but she held his hand where he had placed it on one side of her head.

"Don't go," she pleaded in a whisper. "Please." She was losing control and knew it. The pill was beginning to take effect. "I don't like drugs," she murmured. "Even aspirin."

"Shh, it'll be all right." He cradled her in his arms as she drifted off into a pill-induced sleep.

***

Again she was driving on a road. The scenery was familiar but the atmosphere was different. A storm threatened. The black clouds hovered ominously in the sky above the car. A small lake to her left roiled threateningly. The birds were silent. To her right was the driveway that led to the cottage. She turned in, hoping to find her haven. But for some reason, the car stopped. She couldn't go any farther, nor could she remove herself from the car.

Although she could see the cottage at the end of the driveway, she couldn't get to it. The sun shone brightly in the glade even though the rest of the area was embroiled in a summer storm. She sobbed and tossed and turned in the hot and sweaty car seat, which gradually took on the feel of an arm chair, still damp from her feverish perspiration. Someone was hovering over her.

***

"Jade, Jade, wake up." Jason couldn't take any more of her cries. He had made the coffee and drank most of it himself as he sat and watched Jade go through some torment in the chair. He didn't know what to do. He couldn't leave her alone. He wanted to ask the doctor, who was an old friend of his, but he couldn't get out to telephone. He hesitated to use the radio in his car; any number of people could be tuned in to the frequency, most especially the cousin and his friend, and he definitely did not want to confide in the young officer out front about Jade's problem. If she wanted to tell others, fine, but he would not.

"Jade," he shook her again. Somewhat groggily, she came out of her sleep. "You were dreaming." His black eyes registered his relief as he looked into her green ones. Her eyes were fathomless, and he felt himself being pulled into untold depths. He could become lost in them for endless time.

As Jade looked at him, she felt a peaceful feeling of coming home. She saw in his eyes a caring and tenderness that she had never seen before even in Derek's eyes. Derek hadn't really been anything to her. She knew that now. She had thrown herself at him, looking more for a father figure than a lover. Derek had rejected her physical advances, although he had let her almost live at his apartment. She had felt alone and rejected without him, but also with him. This enigmatic man before her, who still had his hands on her shoulders, made her feel complete . . . almost. She felt that she had known him forever and could trust him always, but she was cautious about letting anyone know how she felt.

Jason handed her a cup of coffee. "Drink this," he said gruffly, looking out the window. The police car was still there, half facing the cottage and half facing the highway. He sat beside her as she drained the last of the liquid from the mug. "Feel like eating now?"

She shook her head. "You go ahead. There should be some food in the fridge. I brought groceries with me."

"Not enough to keep a chicken alive," he told her. "I went out and bought some more food this morning before I went to Tom's. I've already put it away in the fridge and cupboard."

She looked at him, nearly ready to cry. That was something she did only under extreme conditions. The tears welled up and spilled over onto her cheeks.

"Go ahead and cry," he recommended.

Mortified, she said, "If that was supposed to stop me, it did." She laughed. Tentatively she reached for his hand. It was warm. "You're warm," she told him, huskily. "All over. You're a very warm and tender man. Are you married?" she asked, hoping her voice would sound simply polite and not betray her vital interest.

He had never been told that he was warm before, not even by his former wife. The observation shook him. "I was. A long time ago. She died." His terse statements showed her his reluctance to speak about his past, and Jade interpreted this as a sign of his enduring love for his lost wife.

She gasped and looked at him tenderly. "I'm sorry," she whispered.

"Don't be. It was a long time ago, and the marriage was over before she died." He spoke in a matter-of-fact-tone, putting up a barrier between them, pushing her away from him emotionally.

She wanted to ask him more, but felt his reticence. Instead, she leaned over and kissed him on the cheek, astonishing both of them. She laughed, embarrassed. "The pills must be having some sort of effect on my inhibitions. Either that or the injury to my head is still having its effect on some portion of my brain."

For what seemed several moments he just looked at her. Then the next thing she knew she was in his arms. He kissed her lightly on the forehead, a kiss intended to be chaste and comforting, but it didn't stop there. A muffled moan escaped him as he pulled her into his embrace, kissing her warm lips, first gently, then with more fervor. With mounting desire, he pressed her lips open, probing her delicious tongue. She had been kissed that way before, but never had it been like this. She moaned, as her whole body began to respond, and she became one mass of new, fluid sensations. His hand slipped beneath her T-shirt and cupped her lace-covered breast, his thumb caressing her nipple until it strained against her bra. Part of his mind was telling him it was too soon for this, that he shouldn't be doing it, even if it weren't too soon, but he ignored the warning. Jade pushed against him, wanting more. He pulled back.

"This is damn awkward," he muttered. "Let's get

where it's comfortable, and where we aren't on view for the whole bloody police force."

In a daze, she looked up, not remembering the young man in the car. She glanced through the window at the officer, who was trying not to notice what was going on. Her mind didn't register Jason's embarrassment. Her reasoning processes had completely shut down, assaulted by these new overwhelming sensations. Jason half carried her to the rug in front of the unlighted fireplace. The day outside was warm, and so was the cottage, accentuated by the fire of their own emotions. The interruption didn't bother Jade. She was too engrossed in being loved, too eager to continue, to object to the short delay.

On the rug, she wrapped her arms about his neck, feeling the taut muscles of his shoulders. She inhaled the intoxicating mixture of maleness and aftershave lotion. Then she tentatively put her hand under his shirt. His skin was smooth, except between his hardened pecs, where the chest hair felt coarse in her fingers. His well-toned body accentuated his muscles, and she closed her eyes and delighted in the hardened male nipples, surprising herself by her intense desire.

Pushing up his shirt, she followed his lead, and leaning her face against his bare chest, kissed his nipples. He had unsnapped her bra, and she could feel his warm skin against her breasts. His hand moved farther down across her flat stomach, and opening her jeans he caressed her smooth creamy thighs, working his way up to the very soul of her sexual desire. He fondled her until she was writhing out of control; pushing against him wanting more; lifting her hips off the floor. Her hands had wandered all over his warm, tanned body, but she was too new to these sensations, too overcome by her own sexuality so that she whimpered against him, wanting something she couldn't articulate.

In tune with her feelings, he didn't push her. She

moaned as he continued to cradle and kiss her, his breathing erratic. A knock sounded on the cottage door.

"Damn!" he growled ruefully, but at the same time feeling relief. Lifting Jade from the rug, he placed her back in the chair. "Just a minute!" he called out, checking Jade's disheveled appearance and kissing her cheek as he did so. Taking several deep ragged breaths to calm himself, he opened the door to the OPP officer from the car.

"I just wondered if you needed any help," he enquired with a grin splitting his boyish face.

"No, I don't need any help, especially from you," Jason snorted, pulling his T-shirt neatly over his jeans and willing his body to relax.

"Okay, okay," the officer tried vainly to control his grin. "I just figured it was sort of hard trying to keep someone like her under surveillance properly."

"Under surveillance?!" A shrill yelp from Jade startled them both. "You're keeping me under surveillance? Is that what this *concern* of yours is all about?" Her white face registered shock and disbelief. "You're afraid I'm in contact with drug dealers, aren't you? Oh God." She groaned and covered her face with her hands. Her headache returned with a vengeance.

Jason glowered at the intruding officer, who was now unsure of his ground. "She is not under surveillance," he snarled scathingly to the younger man. "We're keeping an eye on her to protect her."

"Sorry. I must have gotten my orders wrong." He backed slowly away from the door.

Jason knew that the man had not misunderstood his orders. Tom's office was probably keeping her under surveillance without telling him. He wondered if Toronto even knew that he was in the vicinity, but they must. Tom had phoned Toronto when Jade had been hit and when the drugs had been found. Jason was sure that Tom would have told them that he was here--even if he was on vacation. Jason remembered that he, himself, had told his captain four days ago where he was going. Now he was in a quandary; as far as he knew he was with Jade to protect her.

He snorted to himself. Some protection. He had damn near raped her just a few minutes ago. And it would have been rape. In the state she was in he doubted if she knew what she was doing, aside from letting her emotions and body take over for her. If she were to take him to court, he knew which party the judge and jury would side with. Damn. He turned back to Jade. She was curled up in the large chair, her white face registering her intense loathing and deep hurt.

"Jade, believe me, I didn't know you were under surveillance. I was just trying to keep an eye on you to see that no harm came to you." Even to him, his explanation sounded hollow, and he wondered if she was thinking along the same lines as himself. She just looked at him mutely, having lapsed into a shocked silence. He had lost her and he knew that wherever she had gone, he couldn't reach her until she had worked through the hurt and betrayal.

Jade was trying with difficulty not to cry. She had thought she had found someone she could trust; she had nearly divulged her history of visions to him, thinking he would understand. She had done it again. All her relationships from day one had been fiascos, with the exception of Aunt Kate, she qualified, forgetting her many friends and her employer who loved her for herself.

"Jade, listen to me." He put his fingers on her chin to turn her face to him. She resisted. "Don't be so bloody pigheaded," he yelled in frustration, more angry with himself than with her. In fact, he was angry with the whole damn situation--the young officer, headquarters, and everybody else involved. Well, at least her apathy had vanished, he noted , as she turned on him like a snake that has had its tail stepped on.

"I'm through letting you help me. Leave me alone," she hissed. "Please!" Tears filled her lovely green eyes and for a moment he was reminded of the hidden depths of oceans, the mystery, the danger, the rapture. She wouldn't let the tears overflow, he knew.

He cursed the officer outside. He denounced the department. He blasphemed the whole situation and Tom for getting him involved in the first place. Even Lorraine's mouth-watering dinner couldn't make up for this. "Jade, please let me take you to somewhere I know you will be safe. Please!" It was his turn to plead with her. His shaking fingers combed through his hair in worry and exasperation.

Looking at the distraught man before her, Jade agreed to his plan. Her aunt's cottage held no safety for her now, and it had lost any enchantment it once had. She hadn't even been to the clearing, her favorite spot, since Jason had cleaned it out for her. It was the remembrance of this help that gradually softened her towards him. She wanted to believe him, wanted to believe he could keep her safe, wanted to believe he was interested in her for herself. Would somebody who was keeping her under surveillance have cut the weeds and overgrowth surrounding the cottage? Would he have come to her rescue and looked so miserable?

"Where?" she enquired warily.

"You'll see. I bet even your headache will disappear when you get there. A very lovely lady will love to look after you."

"Who?" She frowned. A flashback of dream came to her.

"My grandmother," he said softly. She could tell from his tone that he loved this grandmother of whom he now spoke.

"Does she have white hair?" She asked as the image of

the dream woman came back to her.

"Yes." He frowned. "Why?"

But she didn't answer him. She began to feel better. Then the flashback of the storm came to her, the last dream in which she hadn't been able to get to the cottage. She trembled. "We're in for more trouble." She gazed at him with far-seeing eyes. He looked at her, and knew without a doubt that she had what his Scottish grandmother had called *second sight*. He respected this. His other grandmother had the same ability, but called it by its Ojibway name. At the moment, however, he just hoped Jade's powers were inaccurate.

They gathered her few things together in one of her two suitcases and locked the door. Jason went over to have a brief conversation with the officer and to apprize him of some of his plan. The young man listened, thoroughly chastened. He started to apologize to Jason, but the older man cut him short, knowing that no apology was needed. What the officer had thought was only fact. He knew that the man had thought Jason was taking advantage of the suspect. Well, he had been. Hell, a lot of guys did do that; but he didn't. And he didn't want his budding relationship with Jade cheapened by any police locker room jokes or snickering remarks.

Jason didn't tell him where they were going, only that Jade was going to be placed somewhere else. It was the cottage that was under surveillance, he emphasized, and anyone else who came into it. "Keep a sharp lookout," he admonished as he turned from the police car.

There was a problem with what to do with Jade's car. She was unfit to drive, and he didn't want to leave his car there for one minute. There was nothing to do but leave her car for the time being and have Tom come back with him to pick it up. First he would leave Jade with his grandmother. He had no intention of telling anyone where he was taking her. He wouldn't even tell Tom, but he knew that Tom would know. He helped Jade into his car and started to drive farther north toward his grandmother's cottage.

CHAPTER FOUR

Jason's grandmother's cottage was more isolated than the one belonging to Jade's aunt, at least to people who were unfamiliar with the area. In actual fact, it was close to several others, also unseen from the secondary road. A dirt bush road led off from the highway and several cottages nestled beside it, concealed from curious eyes. As long as no one had seen Jason drive away from Jade's cottage, or the direction in which they were going, Jade would be safe with his grandmother. The sky had become overcast, and a summer storm threatened. As was common in this country, the storm could be localized, leaving other areas unaffected, or it could cover the area for kilometers around in drenching torrential rains. Somehow or other, though, Jason knew the sun would be shining at his grandmother's cottage. He had great faith in his decision and in his grandmother.

It always seemed to be shining there, he thought, although rationally, he suspected that it had weathered its fair share of storms, in all senses. His grandmother had not always lived a tranquil life. It certainly hadn't been all that serene when she had helped to raise him. He had been a belligerent and sulky youth, well on the way to what he liked to call his antisocial behavior, when his grandmother had taken over his care. She had raised him with a great deal of love and discipline, especially discipline, he remembered. The beginnings of a smile etched his face as he thought fondly of his youth. All the times he had been at his grandmother's home, it had offered him a shelter, especially in his adult years. His grandmother would never allow him to bring his bitterness into the house.

"Leave it at the highway," she always admonished him, when he made one of his infrequent telephone calls to say he would visit. "I want none of your self-made problems here. This must remain a peaceful place. The spirits love to come here to visit me, but they won't come if there is turmoil in the house. Sometimes my house is much more restful than where they dwell." She would give a playful chuckle. Even though she joked about it with him, never really knowing if he believed or not, she was quite serious about the spirit world. He knew, too, that he could not leave his problems at the highway, and his grandmother did not really expect that he would. It was her way of telling him that he would find peace at the cottage, and he usually did.

He didn't doubt for a minute that some people had the power to see the past or the future, but he put this power down to some sort of innate ability, some intuitive force that came more naturally to some people than to others. Even what he called his gut instinct was related, he supposed, but never would he have said that a spirit was helping him. He wasn't even sure that he wanted help from a spirit. Who was to say that just because a person died, that person knew any more than when he or she had been alive? If a person couldn't manage his life on earth, would he manage living any better in the next realm? Why should transition from this life to the next suddenly make people smarter? Or more lovable? Or more agreeable? No, he preferred to put the power down to some electrical impulse in the brain that wasn't fully understood yet.

He had never told his grandmother this, of course; he probably hadn't ever had a discussion like this with anyone. The only person that he felt he could have this kind of discussion with was now curled up as close to the passenger door as she could get, looking apprehensively out at the scenery and still giving him the silent treatment whenever he tried to start a conversation.

His grandmother's cottage was fifteen kilometers farther north than Jade's, and seven kilometers in on Highway 64, a secondary road that wound for 65 kilometers westward through Field and then to Sturgeon Falls. Set back a short distance from the secondary highway, at the end of the rough bush road, the cottage was difficult to find, especially for anyone not familiar with the area. He drove slowly, not in any hurry to give up his precious cargo just yet. He had warned his grandmother that he might bring Jade to her. Grandmother had smiled enigmatically.

"What are you thinking now, Grandmother?" he had asked tenderly, using an endearing and respectful Ojibway term.

She had just looked at him, assessing his character and capabilities, he surmised. "Have some more coffee. I don't see you so often now that you're a big shot in Toronto."

"You can always come down, you know. It isn't that far, and the bus from Timmins passes twice a day. I've told you that before." He knew, though, that his grandmother preferred to stay in her cottage. At eighty-six, she was not young enough anymore to travel on her own to Toronto, although she would have raised her eyebrows and disputed the notion scoffingly if he had even suggested it. He smiled to himself as he remembered the previous morning's visit to his grandmother, while Jade lay unconscious in Tom's house. In the car, Jade's face still bore signs of her animosity toward him. They drove on in a silence that made each kilometer seem three times as long.

The sun shone brightly, with a sublime light. Grandmother stood in the sunshine in the glade behind her cottage, next to the shimmering brook. The spirit world was more powerful near running water, she knew. The forces gathered strength from the energy of the water and the trees. "Trouble is coming," she said to the man before her.

"Yes, there is no way to prevent it."

"But they must not find this place," she worried. "If there is no way to prevent the trouble, we must see that it happens before Jason nears this place. My house is one of harmony. We cannot have anything sinister or immoral happening here. And more importantly, the evil ones must not know where this cottage is, or they will find the girl here."

He nodded. "Already the car is in pursuit of Jason and the girl. Jason is driving slowly; the other car will catch up to them, unless he decides to drive faster. He might, you know. The atmosphere in the car is not conducive to harmony, *nindikwem*."

She laughed through her tears for her grandson. "It is good to be past the stage when love first bites, is it not?"

He smiled tenderly. "All ages are good, old grandmother. But yes, the world seems more comfortable when we have mellowed a little. I must go now," he told her gently. "The strength is draining from both of us."

She nodded, giving him a reluctant smile. She did not return immediately to the cottage, but lingered in the sun. Regardless of how pleasing her cottage was, she preferred the outdoors. Life was passing too quickly not to take advantage of the fresh air. She stayed in the glade, absorbing the invigorating power of nature. There was another reason she did not want to return to the cottage. She wanted no one to know that the cottage was there, or that there was anything important about that part of the bush. From the road, the track looked just that--a bush trail made by hunters. People from the city would hesitate before taking that rutted track, not knowing where it would end or how much damage it would do to their vehicle. The men pursuing Jason had murder on their minds, she knew. They must not come anywhere near her property. If it was Jason's and Jade's destiny that they had to meet up with the men, then it must be so, but the meeting had to be precipitated before they reached the cottage.

She hoped the spirit world would perform well. There was nothing more she could do, except send fervent thoughts toward her grandson. She wished she had remembered to bring a thermos of tea with her into the glade. Her memory seemed to be slipping lately. "What good are powers when memory is going?" she quietly asked a red oak tree, but she needed no answer. Her life work was nearly done. She loved this place. She reflected on her life as she rested against a white birch tree, which now leaned over the small stream. Once, it had stood tall and straight, a sentinel of the glade. She looked at it now, nostalgically. The birch was old like her. It would soon be time for the tree to fall completely to provide for new growth, just as it was time for her to let go and let others take over. Soon she could go to the spirit world. Not yet, though, so she must not be careless. She closed her eyes, secure in the knowledge that she was safe in the glade.

As Jason drove, he suddenly lost control of the steering. "No," he exclaimed aloud, "not a flat tire! Not now." He pulled over to the shoulder of the highway. The front tire on the passenger side was deflating rapidly.

Well, he had a spare, so he would just have to make the best of a bad deal. Cursing and muttering under his breath, he turned to look at Jade. She appeared tired and drained, her skin white beneath the little tan that she had. He noticed her swallow convulsively, and he wanted to take her in his arms and comfort her. Instead, he queried, "Jade?"

Turning to face him, she looked straight at him, but her

eyes were not focusing. "Something is wrong. I can feel it. The air sparks with danger. It isn't the flat tire. That's nothing." She had changed flat tires herself. No, something made her neck prickle and beat a tattoo of fear down her spine. Just as Jason opened the car door to have a look at the tire, a Ford Fiesta drove up beside them. It was the same car that had driven into Jade's drive three days before. In it were two men. Jason recognized the slightly-built, dark driver as the one who had asked for Rick. Before he had time to ask him if he had found the man he was looking for, Jade exclaimed, "Rick!"

Jason frowned. Jade's attention was directed toward the younger man with shoulder length, unkempt blond hair. Jason, his senses alert, didn't like the looks of the man, and thought he looked familiar, but couldn't place him. Obviously, Jade knew him.

"Jason, this is my cousin Rick. What are you doing up here, Rick?" She turned to the man before her. He looked tougher than she remembered him; he had lost his boyishness and the petulance that she remembered so well. Now there was a hardness about him that she couldn't comprehend. "Why didn't you come to the cottage?" she continued. "I've cleaned it all up. Don't forget, it's your cottage."

Rick replied by giving a cynical snort. Jade frowned, but said pleasantly, "Who's your friend?" Was this the sensitive boy she had always known? She looked from him to the other man, seeing only two scruffy, hostile men in front of her.

"I'm Len." The darker man identified himself by his first name only.

She didn't know about the other man's reasons for being hostile, but there was no reason that she knew for Rick to have such an attitude. Remembering a conversation with her aunt, Jade knew that Rick had dropped out of college, and she wondered if his reasons for quitting school were the same as for his choice of friends and his disreputable appearance. In an act of delayed adolescence, he was showing society that he could make independent decisions. She turned toward Jason and noticed his puzzled frown. What was it he saw? she wondered. She knew that he would not be seeing the same man as she saw, meshed with and superimposed upon the boy of the past.

Suddenly she experienced a fragment of flashback. Nothing concrete, just a hand reaching for her, and her being pushed onto the floor. She tried to grasp the picture, bring it into focus, but it eluded her effort.

"Mother gave it to you," he snarled, interrupting her perusal of him. "Although I don't know why. You've been a loser since day one."

She stepped back in shock, but gathered her resources quickly, dismissing the urge to demand an explanation. "Rick? I don't understand. The cottage isn't mine. I told Aunt Kate years ago that it should go to her own family."

"I thought it was already in your name."

Jade could have sworn that he turned a little pale when she shook her head in the negative. He definitely looked uncomfortable with the information. "You mean it's still in Mother's name?"

She nodded as she explained how she felt about Kate's offering of the cottage.

"How about going back there, then, for a chat?" He had quickly switched to a more coaxing tone. "I haven't seen you in ages." Wondering about his mercurial shift in mood, she turned to Jason who was sizing up the two men and, by the look on his face, not liking at all what he was seeing.

He was trying to figure out why the two men were this side of Jade's cottage, and wondered if the men had been watching all their movements. His quiet, authoritative voice broke into her indecision. "I think we should just continue on our way. We want to get to New Liskeard before the storm hits."

"New Liskeard? I didn't realize we were going to New Liskeard." She frowned and caught a cautionary glance from him. From the alert expressions of her cousin and his friend, the interchange had not gone unnoticed by the two men. Jason was trying to warn her, she could feel it, but something in her rebelled at what she perceived as his trying to control her. She wasn't about to be bullied by him any longer. She was still miffed at him for keeping her under surveillance, even though he had denied any knowledge of it.

Refusing to think anything good of Jason at the moment and wondering why he should warn her about her cousin, she told him adamantly, "I'm going back with Rick." A tiny smile pulled at her lips. Smugly she realized that she had thoroughly exasperated the macho cop before her. He was not going to dictate what she should or should not do, she fumed quietly. At the same time she acknowledged an inner warning not to let Rick and his friend know of any animosity between her and Jason. "I should pick up my own car, anyway."

There was nothing Jason could do. He didn't want the two men to know that he was a detective. And he knew that with the officer outside the cottage, Jade would be relatively safe. Now that he wasn't taking Jade to his grandmother's cottage, he considered going to North Bay, so that he could glean more information. It had been singularly unforthcoming up to now. He wanted to speak to Jade privately to apprise her of his whereabouts, and stepped over to her, but Rick, forestalling any such circumstance, had taken her by the arm and almost dragged her into their car. Although his actions had appeared rough, Jade had seemingly acquiesced. Short of pulling out his credentials and demanding her release to him, Jason was restricted in his effort to get close to her.

Revealing his identity would not do any good at this point. It would conceivably only scare the men off temporarily. Although this seemed personally a good thing, Jason, with his years of training and experience vetoed the plan. If he or Jade lost sight of them, it could be months or maybe years before they found them again.

At the moment, Jade seemed to prefer to go with them rather than with him, anyway. He let her go, silently willing her not to mention that he was with the police department. By the time the black Ford drew away, he had finished changing the tire, and he drove quickly to North Bay, staying behind the Ford until it turned into Jade's cottage.

Fortunately, because of the relocation of the Ontario Provincial Police station, he wasn't forced to negotiate city traffic. When he had called Tom's home number on his car phone to let him know what was going on, Tom had assured him that although the police officer who was doing the surveillance was young and somewhat brash, he was quite good at his job. Jason snorted at the memory of the morning. It seemed ages ago that it had all taken place. He didn't think much of the officer doing surveillance duty, but Tom knew him better than he did. Tom had chuckled when Jason enlightened him as to the events of the morning.

"What's so funny?" Jason had snarled into the mouthpiece..

"You," Tom had replied. "But I know you don't think it's funny. Ah, well, I was there once myself. It's just taken you longer to reach this point. You've had a few detours on the way. Don't worry, my detachment will keep an eye on Jade and the cottage and her cousin and the kid on surveillance," he had assured Jason.

"You could be a little more serious about it," Jason had growled, only to hear Tom's laughter in reply.

Jason swung into the parking lot of the new building. The men and the one woman on duty were very helpful after he had shown them his credentials. He knew that

Tom would have phoned the office to make sure that he got all the help he needed. They had known about the homicide, of course, but they had not known about the drugs, until Jason's disclosure. This surprised him. He was astonished to learn that the drug trade was a thriving business in the North Bay area. Why hadn't Tom let his staff know about the drugs sooner?

He speculated about his friend's action and possible repercussions. Tom was taking a big risk if he had failed to report the cocaine and marijuana find to protect Jade. He obviously had a great deal of faith in her, a faith that for all Jason's desire, was lacking in him. Tom had known, after Jason had informed him of the details, of Jade's escapade in Toronto and that she had been cleared of the charges against her. Tom had accepted all this at face value; Jason had searched for a missing piece to the puzzle.

He stayed at the police station for what seemed like hours, first on the phone to Toronto, then filling in the North Bay detachment on all that was going on. The only thing he left out was his strengthening involvement with Jade. He knew how that would go down with headquarters--a girl, cleared of drug charges, but whose cottage was filled with packages of cocaine and marijuana with a market value of close to a million dollars. His head would be on the chopping block. He had been thinking of asking to be put officially on the case, but then had changed his mind. If he were on the case legitimately, he would have to follow rules. This way, all he had to do was keep a low profile.

He could do more to help the young woman whom he had met only four days before, and who had somehow insinuated her way into the void of his life if he remained outside of officialdom. He was loath to admit it, but he had spent more time thinking about her in the past four days, than he had thinking of Tom's problem with the homicide.

When he told the Toronto office about her cousin, he was informed that was why they had been interested in Jade in the first place, besides her connection to Derek. They had felt there was a close connection between Jade and the two men. Jason tried to get in touch with the people who had handled the case, but to his annoyance, he was told that they were on holiday. There was something about the whole thing that was not adding up. "What about this Derek fellow?" he asked the person on the other end of the line.   There was a silence and then a noncommittal answer.

"You will have to wait for my superiors to come back, for that information," the woman on the Toronto end advised him blandly. He did a slow burn, recognizing the run-around, and was about to denounce the whole system to the ear at the other end of the phone, when he remembered with some chagrin that he, too, was part of that system. It was possible that some of the key personnel were on holiday; hell, he was on vacation himself. He did cull the tidbit that Toronto figured Rick for only a small time dealer. They were keeping him on the loose, hoping to get to the top man of his supply source. Who the other man with Rick was, they didn't know for certain, but felt he was just a lackey. No more information was forthcoming from the personnel in Toronto. Jason rung off, having supplied them with the licence number and the make of the car.

He glanced at his watch and saw with a slight shock that it was after four o'clock. The picture of Jade with the two men sent chills down his spine, and he hurried back to Marten River. He wanted to go straight to Toronto, to be right there so that he could put his thoughts in order, but now was not the time. Until he was certain that Jade was okay, he wouldn't even be in any condition to drive to Toronto, he thought with some dismay. He raced back up the highway, faster than Jade had been going when he had

stopped her for speeding. He felt, however, that he was
quite justified in traveling well over the speed limit. He
wondered fleetingly how many other speeding drivers
thought they, too, were justified in speeding.

Jade, still suffering from the concussion and the shock of
the morning, had allowed herself to be pushed roughly into
the back seat of Rick's car. Immediately after she had
ignored Jason's warning, she regretted it. She wondered
again about her cousin. Was this the young man she had
known as she was growing up? He was changed,
hardened. In fact, she was frightened of him, but
marshaling all her resources, she refused to let her fear
show. Instead, she concentrated on not vomiting all over
their car. At the best of times, she could not sit in the back
seat. With a concussion, it was even worse.

They drove to the cottage where the young police
constable was still on surveillance. At least he was holding
to his job, Jade noticed. As yet, she had no strong fears for
her safety. She did not really think that her cousin would
hurt her, especially in his mother's cottage.

Rick, obviously on edge from seeing the constable,
snarled at her from the front seat. "What the hell is he
doing here? Make like everything is okay," he ordered her.
"I don't want any nosy cops around."

She nodded mutely, wondering why he had felt the need
to admonish her to say everything was all right. Her head
was still aching and her stitched scalp was sore. This
wasn't turning out to be the soothing heart-healing
vacation she had planned from her Toronto apartment, she
mused as the three of them exited the car and proceeded to
the front door.

The OPP constable walked over to them, alert to all
nuances of body language and weighing up the situation.
Jade introduced her cousin and "his friend, Len" from
Toronto. The officer, intuiting that something was amiss,

was about to ask where she had left the detective sergeant, but he got no further than "Where's . . . ." when he noticed the instant flash of alarm in Jade's eyes. He said only, "If you need me, just call."

Once they were inside, Rick turned on her sharply. "What the hell is that all about?"

"I don't know," Jade replied wearily. "All I know is that there were drugs stashed in the cottage, I was knocked out, and there has been a homicide in the area, and the police seem to think there is some connection." It was a capsulated version of the events of the past few days, but at the moment it was all Jade felt capable of giving. She was going to suggest making coffee so that she could sit down and relax, but as she looked over to the two men she was startled to discover that they did not seem to be surprised by her mention of the drugs, or of the murder, but rather were assessing the situation between them.

"You know about it!" she exclaimed. "You know about the drugs, don't you? Rick, did you hide them here? Did you break the window? What is going on? Rick, what has happened to you?"

Her series of short questioning outbursts were met by a derisive snort from Len. "Why do people always think that somethin' happened to you? Maybe he's been rotten from day one," he smirked, his head bobbing from Rick to Jade and back. "You should have hit her harder with that iron. Or maybe you shouldn't have hit her at all. There're other ways to keep her quiet. This here's one cool chick, this cousin of yours. Looks like she could do with a good lay."

As Jade gasped indignantly, Rick glared at the smaller but older man. "Shut up!" Seeing the awareness in Jade's eyes, he must have decided that denial would be useless. "Yeah, I know about it. Len and I watched that guy carry you out to his car. Is he your current lay? We watched him carry our stash out too. Come to think of it, your boyfriend couldn't have been all that worried about you if he stopped to pick up the coke and pot, too. With what we brought up from Toronto this trip, we could have been set for a few years. Now you've gone and spoiled our plans. You could have been in on our little deal, but no, you mess up again" He looked at her in mock pity. "The poor born loser, eh Jade?"

"What has changed you?" She frowned, trying to figure him out. "And why are you so upset that Aunt Kate would leave me the cottage? Your parents made sure that you had enough. Your sisters didn't mind when she offered me the cottage." She pondered this now, through the haze that her headache produced. Maybe she had been wrong about all of them; it certainly wouldn't have been the first error in judgement she had made regarding people, she mused. And it wasn't her last, either, judging by Derek and now this new cop--surveillance, indeed!

"But maybe I did mind," he pointed out. "And now, unfortunately for you, you're with us whether you like it or not. We've been keeping an eye on you ever since you got mixed up with that drug dealer in Toronto. For a time we thought that maybe you could come in with us. But we changed our minds. Obviously, little Miss Goody-Two Shoes, here, is too naive and squeaky clean," he mocked. "Cleared by the police and under no suspicion." Jade recognized the headline from one of the Toronto papers. "By the way, who is that guy you were with? If he's your lover, honey, he sure doesn't have your well-being on his mind. Or maybe it's not *your well-being* he cares about. Maybe it's his, if you get my drift." Just in case she didn't, he let his eyes wander to her pubic area. He laughed at her look of disgust. When she didn't answer, he continued. "We can take care of you, no problem. My mother will believe that you've followed in your parents' footsteps and have gone off the deep end. She'll worry for a while, wondering if she could have helped you more. You know how she frets like an old mother hen, but after a bit, she won't bother to look out for you. Too bad that Len, here, thought the other girl was you. But that's the way these things happen." He spoke with no show of remorse and Jade shuddered, both intrigued by and appalled at his lack of emotion.

Rick continued in a cold, matter-of-fact voice. "You should have been dead a long time ago. Just think, you wouldn't have had any more problems. You wouldn't have to keep running to my mother every time you mess up. Face it, Jade, you're not fit to live anyway. You have to be tough to live in this world, and you're not. Now, I, on the other hand, have learned to survive and to enjoy it. It's a dog-eat-dog world, and right now we're the dogs doin' the eating. Len and I had a nice set-up here. No one would have thought to look in this cottage for drugs, but you had to come along and stick your nose into things." His arm snaked out and grabbed her, his voice rising an octave in his agitation. "You never answered me." He grabbed her by the hair, wrenching her neck and parting her scalp wound. "Who's the guy?"

For a minute she debated whether or not she should tell him. Then the thought occurred to her that if she did acknowledge Jason as a cop, he would panic and run from there. She tried it. "He's a detective sergeant from Toronto," she stated defiantly. "He's up here checking into the murder of that poor girl."

His face stilled. "A cop?"

"Hey, Rick, we ain't shooting no cop," Len sputtered. "We can get rid of this broad easy, but we ain't shooting no cop. And we can't kill her here. We gotta clear out."

Rick surprised Jade by agreeing. She knew that under different circumstances, he would have had no qualms about shooting an officer, but without Len's support, he was nothing but empty taunts and threats, a weak man, she realized now. But weak men could be the most dangerous and the most unstable.

Rick now grabbed Jade by the throat, shaking her, ridding himself of all the built-up hostilities he had been harboring toward her over the years. She had never felt that she had been encroaching on any of her cousins' territory when she had gone to her aunt with problems. But now she wondered whether the other cousins didn't feel as Rick did. She forced her mind to the present, not a hard thing to do with the violent man who still had his grip around her throat. What was she to do? He was now nearly out of control, so she would have to be careful. He shoved her onto the floor and held her down with his booted foot. "Want to have some fun with her, Len?"

She wanted to scream and plead with them to leave her alone, but that would inflame Rick even more. She thought of the officer outside, but hesitated about calling out to him for aid. Belatedly, she had realized that both Len and Rick carried guns. And regardless of Len's statement to the contrary, she had no doubt that one or both of the men would shoot when confronted by the officer. Len seemed to be more in control of his emotions and actions, but in some ways that was even more chilling. There wasn't much of a choice between a hot-headed killer and a remorseless one. Dead was dead.

A scene from the past flicked through her mind. It was of Rick at a very early age killing a bird *because he felt like it,* watching its agony as he pulled each wing off, as he punctured each eye socket. She had fled behind a bush and vomited. When Rick had found her, he had grabbed her arms and threatened to kill her as he had the bird, if she should tell anyone. Another picture of Rick juxtaposed itself with the previous one--an enraged Rick when Aunt Kate had said "no" to him. She couldn't even remember what the episode had been about, but she remembered she had been there to witness Rick's wrath and frustration. Even as a young boy he had experienced problems, she realized now--maybe even more problems than she had.

Maybe he had needed his mother more than she. Jade began to feel sorry for him, even when he gave her ribs a nudge with his boot.

When he grabbed her T-shirt and hauled her to her feet, however, her sympathy dissipated. She hoped she didn't let on how relieved she was that he had not given Len time to rape her.

"You're nothing but a sucky bitch," he railed at her, keeping his voice under a semblance of control. "You're not worth wasting any time over."

"Rick, they'll trace her killing to us," Len spoke urgently. "Even if we don't touch the cop outside, even if we leave here and kill her somewhere else, they will eventually trace it back to us. Too many people know what we look like." His reasoning seemed to sink into Rick's tortured mind. Len pushed his point home. "They won't be able to pin that other girl on us. All they know is that we're into a little trafficking."

"We can't leave her alive here, either," Rick persisted. "She knows too much about us. Come on, bitch. We're just going to have to take you with us, for now. Get some clothes so the cops will think you came with us willingly; maybe we can use you yet, or at least put some of the blame on you to show that you're not so pure as people think." He shoved her into the bedroom to pack.

Jade pulled her suitcase towards her in a daze. She was at a loss as to what to do. Instinct told her that if she signaled the police officer outside, it would be the end of both the officer and her. Even when she had come up to the cottage, and had been at a low point, she had never thought of taking her life. *Or of letting anyone else take it,* she whispered to herself as she gathered some scattered clothes and snapped her suitcase shut. Things were not over yet. She was still in fighting form. And by God, she would fight him until she had no strength left.

For some perverse reason, she now wanted Jason--

desperately. Things would have been different had he been there, she knew. One woman could not overpower two men like those before her. Under average circumstances, she might have taken them both on, but with her head still pounding and Rick on the verge of a volatile eruption, she didn't dare. She knew Jason would have had more resources at his command. Well, there was no use fretting about it. Jason wasn't there. Where had he gone? He had seemed rather ambivalent when her cousin had shown up. On the one hand, he had been nonchalant, and on the other, suspicious.

What kind of police officer was he? He should have known better than to have let her go with Rick and Len. She displaced her anger at her situation onto Jason--to the detriment of his character-- knowing, as she was mentally calling him every name she could think of, that it was completely ridiculous for her to feel that way. After all, he had tried to warn her. He had said they were going to New Liskeard, and she had felt that was a ploy to mislead her cousin. She didn't know exactly where his grandmother's cottage was, but felt sure that it was much closer to Marten River than New Liskeard. Maybe he did discern more than she gave him credit for, so after she had spent some of her anger and frustration, she grudgingly acknowledged that perhaps his intentions were good.

She realized that she was beginning to rely on him the way she had wanted to rely on Derek, and this scared her. She made herself think again of Jason in a less admiring light. Jason had pretty well acted the same way as Derek had. He hadn't said "Get lost, Kid," not in so many words, but he might as well have, she fumed silently. After all, if her cousin hadn't come along, Jason would have foisted her off on his grandmother. Here she was, not being fair to him again, she admonished herself as she wavered between liking him and loathing him, wanting him, not wanting him.   He had looked after her when she had been unconscious, and he had seemed solicitous of her welfare. Rick was right when he said she was screwed up. Her cousin materialized in her bedroom and put an end to her confused and rambling thoughts. He pulled her roughly into the living room.

"Listen, bitch," Rick's voice penetrated her thoughts. "When we go out of here, act natural. If the cop asks where we're going, say you have to get back to Toronto."

Jade wondered why he hadn't asked about her car, so she brought it up herself. "What about my car? It's going to look pretty suspicious if I leave it here. They will know that I wouldn't go back to Toronto without my car." She didn't know what she had gained by saying this. She had thought vaguely that it might deter the two men from doing anything with her.

Rick's eyes widened. "You may be right," he conceded. "You'll just have to come with me, and Len will drive your car." She tried to show no emotion as they secreted their guns in their pockets.

Len looked at him doubtfully. "How about me driving your cousin, in your car?" He smiled self-complacently. "And you take her car. That way, we'll all be happy. Her car is faster, just the way you like it, and I just might have some fun with this cute broad."

"Sure." Rick agreed with more alacrity than Jade would have liked. "A little fun might shake the bitch up a bit. But if you get the chance, you can complete what you should have done months ago. I still don't like having her around."

Jade shuddered. Within a short time, her predicament had become far more serious. They were both mad. Or both had very large chips on their shoulders. Funny, in all the years of her growing up, she had never thought to blame anyone else for her mistakes. That was one thing her parents had taught her at a young age. Young people are supposed to make mistakes. That's the way to learn. But she wasn't to blame others for her errors in judgement. It was only when she went to the psychologist that she was told that her lack of proper parenting had been the cause of her problems. Even now, though, she couldn't stomach foisting all the blame on her parents or on anybody. They had coped with their problems to the best of their ability, even if that ability was seriously flawed.

Their inability to manage without the alcohol was not the cause of Jade's problems, regardless of the psychologist's observations. Her parents had never hinted that she was to blame for anything either. In fact, in between the shouting matches and the drinking bouts, they had been more than willing to make things up to her. She wondered, after the sessions, why she hadn't turned out to be a manipulator or an alcoholic, but she hadn't. She was sure of that.

She and Len were soon on their way down the highway in the black car. It had not been easy to get past the officer with the tale that she had decided to return to Toronto, but after several astute questions, he finally let them go. She hoped he would phone the office or someone immediately after their departure.

Just before they had driven out the driveway, Rick told Len that he would go north and cut off Highway 11 to take secondary Highway 64 across to Field. This would eventually lead him out to Highway 17 at Sturgeon Falls, and he would pass through North Bay from a route that he didn't think the police would look at, at least until he was well out of the area.

He figured he would be past North Bay before anyone started looking for the cherry-red sports car. Len could take his time traveling more slowly down Highway 11 with Jade. If Jason were driving on Highway 11, they thought he would be less likely to notice the Ford Fiesta than Jade's red car, although neither of the men made the mistake of underestimating him.

Rick sped ahead, enjoying the sophisticated handling of Jade's small car. Soon he was out of sight. Len preferred to drive his slower car, seeming to relish being alone with Jade. It was the same car he had driven when he had come searching for Rick three days ago. Was it only four days ago that she had left Toronto? Things had happened so quickly that linear time became nonexistent. Everything blurred into one--past, present, future. Well, lately the future hadn't been coming in so clearly--almost as if there were electrical interference.

Her images reminded her of the times she had watched television in her North York apartment during a thunder storm. The program would fade in and out until it sometimes finally faded out altogether, leaving a blipping screen and staccato beats of static. Jade felt as she thought the TV screen must feel, her head full of static. Images were coming to her but they weren't making any sense. The dream cottage kept fading in and out of her mind without any assistance from her. In fact, she had no control over the images at all. Her headache was returning with a vengeance. She would have given anything to just lean back in the seat and relax, but she was too keyed up and afraid of the man beside her.

As if sensing her thoughts, he now reached over and rubbed his fingers across her breasts. She shuddered in revulsion. "What's wrong, baby, I'm not good enough for you?" he sneered. "Rick said you thought you were too good for a guy."

Her stomach tied itself into knots; she felt nauseated and fought to control it. She knew if she upset him, he would become more obnoxious. She doubted that he really wanted to rape her--and rape would be what it was, she thought. There was no way that she would ever give in to him. She had a small hope that he was just playing with her sadistically, as a cat plays with a mouse until the mouse frightens itself to death. She was no mouse. She was not going to frighten herself to death. She sensed that he had more on his mind than sex. Probably he was thinking of that other woman he had killed and also her own death, or maybe for him sex and killing were inextricably intertwined. A chill rippled through her.

"Why did you have to kill that other woman?" she asked him. Suddenly she had a strong urge to know.

He laughed harshly. "Too bad. It was your cousin's idea to kill you, you know, but he left me to do the actual deed. He ain't got the guts for it. Hey, what the hell, once you kill one person, it's easy to kill another, and another. The great sex beforehand didn't hurt any, either." He giggled. When he turned toward her to gauge her reaction, her stricken face made him laugh even louder.

She gulped and shook her head. "I never thought that I intruded upon their life that much. But why her? What does or did she have to do with me?"

"Case of mistaken identity, baby. Rick was using the cottage when he spotted this doll walking along by the driveway. He panicked. One, because we had bags of coke and pot stashed there; two, because he thought it was you and it suddenly came to him that he could get rid of you and no one would know the difference; and three, he knew nobody but you and his mother used the cottage, and his mother was in Florida." He laughed again, and placed his hand roughly on her thigh.

"Relax, Honey. Rick said he tried to get it on with you once, but you smashed him in the face. Not your type, eh? I don't want to kill you yet. Maybe if you're good, I won't have to kill you at all. Rick's gone in the other direction. He won't be worrying about us for a while. He knows I want to lay you."

"I don't think you do," she said with more confidence than she felt. "I think it's all an act." She tried to make her voice sound relatively normal as she forced her mind to dredge up hidden memories. When Len had mentioned

Rick's attempt to have sex with her, she had shivered, but had been unable to summon up any concrete detail.

"Don't kid yourself. I ain't had a good lay in ages, and you look ready for one, especially when you know I'll probably off you sometime after. It adds to the thrill."

Without warning, her stomach heaved. "Stop the car!" She cried out, putting her hand over her mouth.

Seeing her white face, he brought the car to a squealing standstill along the shoulder. "Shit! Don't puke all over my car or I'll off you now."

She wasn't listening.   She recognized a massive outcropping of red granite rock that she had seen when she had driven this way before.   From years ago she remembered that there was a bog close to the highway in this spot. There were bogs all along this highway, some close to the road, others back in the bush. Now an idea suddenly occurred to her, but first she had to vomit up the contents of her stomach. She felt reviled. Len's advances certainly weren't anywhere near Jason's.   Len's were packed with lust and hatred. She hadn't felt this revulsion at noon when Jason had lovingly caressed her. Her whole body shuddered; her skin tightened and turned clammy. She wrenched open the car door and got out quickly.

Where was Jason? He had said that she would be looked after.   He wasn't doing a particularly good job at the moment. Then she remembered that she had told him that she didn't need anyone to look after her, that she was quite capable of looking after herself. Hah, that was a laugh. She was getting in thicker and thicker. If anyone had believed her before about not being involved with drugs, and not knowing that Derek was a drug dealer, they sure wouldn't believe her now when she was with her cousin and his so-called friend.

"Jeeze, hurry up, will ya!" Len came to the back of the car to check on her.

"Just give me a minute," she hiccupped.

Looking at the vomited contents of her stomach all over the shoulder of the road, he turned quickly to return to the driver's side but was halted by her question. "Have you got any wipes or a cloth with you?"

He hadn't. She felt his eyes on her as she reached into her suitcase and took out a T-shirt, then began to peel off her soiled one. Good thing she hadn't eaten any lunch, she thought. What she had brought up was her breakfast from hours ago. She caught his eyes on her breasts as she pulled off her T-shirt, and her idea suddenly formed more intensively. "I think there's a small pool of water just behind that rock. Just let me rinse myself off, then I'll be back."

A moment's doubt flickered across his face. Then it passed when he looked at her breasts. She had worn a bra, but now it was wet with vomit, so she removed it, first because it was uncomfortable, and second, to distract Len. She dared a darting glance his way as she bent to unhook her bra. Apparently her ploy was working. His look of doubt had turned to one of complete lust.

"Make sure you get all your spilled guts off, Babe." He flicked her nipple, which stubbornly stayed flat. Her lack of response angered him, and he suddenly lashed out and struck her face. "Get moving! You've got five minutes. Then when you get back, I'll show you a bang-up party." He undulated his hips to emphasize what he was saying.

Jade, clutching the two T-shirts, scurried across the flat red granite rock, her face stinging. The sky darkened, and the rain, which had been threatening all day, began to descend in a light drizzle. She paused as if looking for water. In all the years that she had been coming up to the north country, she had done a lot of exploring. The woods did not frighten her at all. She had made it a priority to understand the bush and the animals, so that if she came upon anything out of the ordinary she would know what to do. The only things that terrified her were snakes. On the premise that if she did not see them they wouldn't see her, she did not look for them. Nevertheless, she knew that the boggy area where she now stood would be a good spot to find them. She shucked the image from her mind. There were bigger problems than garter snakes to deal with. The man by the road was a more poisonous serpent. She turned around to see if he was watching. He was. Lifting her hand as if to point that the water she was looking for was just a short distance away, she dropped down out of sight behind the red rock.

CHAPTER FIVE

She had to work quickly, because she had no doubt that he would come looking for her. When he did come, she was counting on knowing the bush better than he did. *Please, God, please God,* she caught her breath on a sob. *Please let me get away from him. Please*! She couldn't say whether the prayer was to an omnipotent deity or to a higher self; she believed in it, had seen the power of it, and used it. Now, she prayed intensely that she would escape from this man and her cousin, and anyone else who thought she was involved with drugs or drug dealers.

The sky continued to darken as more rain clouds gathered force over the hills. It was still afternoon, but grey sky had shaded to late evening black, with rain showers intensifying at intervals to torrential force. Soon she would have complete darkness on her side. She didn't know where she was, exactly, or what she would do, but she was certain that she could not return to her aunt's cottage. There was no telling what or who she would find there.

The OPP constable might still be there, or perhaps Jason would be there. There was also the chance that Rick or Len or both of them might return if they couldn't find her in the bush. Taking a deep breath and exhaling slowly, she let go of her rational thinking and let her instinct for survival take over. She was glad she was wearing her Nike Air shoes. True, she should have been wearing her hiking boots for the bush, but at least the sports shoes afforded her better protection than her sandals would have.

Swiftly she pulled the clean T-shirt over her soiled one. She would need them both. Even though it was summer, the northern nights could turn cold quite suddenly, especially with the rain and lack of sun. Besides, the shirts would be protection against the blackflies and mosquitoes that she was sure to encounter. She pulled her socks up over the legs of her jeans as further protection against the swarms of insects. There wasn't too much she could do about her arms or about her swollen face and scalp wound, all of which were magnets to the insects searching for a blood meal. She would just have to make the best of it. The sporadic rain momentarily eased.

She heard Len slam the car door. "Where are you, you little bitch? Hurry up." Like a startled fawn she was off through the bush. She might not be part Ojibway, as Jason was, but at the moment, spurred onwards by fear and desperation, she doubted that anyone could go through the bush any faster than she. Making as little noise as possible, she cut through the undergrowth, getting as far away from the highway as she could. Eventually she would go back to the road, perhaps farther south. If she turned north now, she would come out on Aunt Kate's property, and there she would not be safe at all. There was no doubt that both Rick and Len would know that land as well as she did.

With the sky darkening even more, she knew she couldn't go too far into the bush, because she really would get lost. She skirted the boggy area and disappeared into the thick undergrowth. With the overcast sky, she had no way of positioning herself by the sun. How deeply into the bush she had traveled she didn't know, but it was a considerable distance before she felt safe enough to stop for a rest. Dampness, humidity, fear. The sweat ran down her face and plastered her hair to her forehead and neck. Her T-shirts clung damply to her and her rain-soaked jeans began to chafe her legs. The salty sweat was attracting the blackflies and mosquitoes, and on the parts of her that weren't covered, the insects found a deep well of rich Nordic blood. She wasn't too worried about the mosquito bites. In this part of the world they didn't carry malaria, and she doubted the west Nile virus had surfaced this far north. The blackflies were another matter. For all the years that she had lived in the North and for all the many visits when she had come to Aunt Kate's cottage, she had never built up an immunity to them. Soon she would be covered in welts she knew. Her face was puffy from Len's infuriated slap, and her left eye had swollen shut. Blood trickled from her scalp wound, but she was alive--so far.

As protection against the invading insects, she now tucked her shirts into her jeans, something she had forgotten to do when she had set out. Hiding behind a huge pine tree, she gasped for breath as silently as she could. The woodland silence was broken only by the rain dripping from the thick branches. She heard no footfalls, but she could not trust to the supposition that Len might not know this part of the bush. It was possible he knew it as well as or better than she.

The black shadowy trees in the under story of the bush caused her no apprehension, and the red spotted, blue-green moss dotting the tree trunks added a familiar touch of color even in the gloom. She looked up. Through the canopy of the overhead leaves, she could see that it was starting to rain again. If the rain kept up, Len would not come very far into the bush. He would not put himself out that much for Rick, but would probably get back into the car and race to catch up with her cousin. Rick, leaving the dirty work to someone else, thought that everything was taken care of. But that someone else wasn't going to get himself soaked to please Rick.

Perhaps Rick had been like that all his life. Well, things were not going to work out for him this time, she reflected. She would give him a run for his money. Not knowing why, she was suddenly inspired to climb the tree that was sheltering her.

The lowest limb was a distance from the ground. She jumped for it. It was beyond her reach. Her fingers scraped the rough bark and blood trickled down her hand. In panic, she sprang for it again, just barely managing to catch the lower branch and with some difficulty to haul herself up into the lower limbs. She rested a moment to regain her breath. The tree was a dense, long-needled white pine, one of very few in this particular area. At some time, the top had been struck by lightning, and the tree, instead of growing upward, continued to expand and spread outward in many overlapping branches. Most of this area was maple and birch; the few spruce trees were spindly and devoid of many needles. This pine was an anomaly. Her guardian angel was looking out for her.

Rain pelted down. She forced herself to climb to the fullest part of the tree. Although she was protected from the pounding rain, she was being drenched from the water dripping from the needles. Looking down, she noticed that the undergrowth had eased back. The rain fell steadily, and the ground below soaked up the water and filled in her footprints. No one would be able to tell that she had been standing there.

She thought she heard a branch snap, but could see no one. Then she heard a louder noise and looked down, trying not to choke on the breath caught in her throat. Len *had* followed her into the bush. He had more grit than she'd given him credit for. Either that, or he feared Rick's wrath more than getting wet. But whether or not he had actually followed her path or had just happened to end up in this spot, Jade wasn't sure. She could just barely see him through the thick branches below her, but she was sure he wouldn't be able to see her if he happened to look up--which he did. She saw him glance at the lower branch which was just out of reach of his extended arm. As Len looked up, peering into the branches, the rain caught him full in the face and she saw him close his eyes against the stinging drops. He looked down at his feet, now sinking into a sodden mass of thick moss and shook his head hard enough to shed the rain water from his hair. Undecided whether to go on or turn back, he looked at his watch. Jade was wearing one too, but had forgotten about it. Now, she didn't chance looking at hers.

She didn't dare move a muscle for fear of giving away her position. The rain eased off slightly while he stood there, just enough to allow the blackflies to come out in hordes after their new victim. She watched him brush at his arms and face and then his arms again, cursing as he did so. Seeming to make up his mind, he turned and started back out of the bush towards the highway.

Len wouldn't take the chance of leaving the car beside the highway too long. Sooner or later the police would pass by and investigate. She didn't think this would happen soon, however, and speculated fleetingly just how far Rick had traveled and whether he was wondering where they were. He was probably gloating over how easily he had distanced himself from what was likely happening to her. If Len got rid of her while Rick was miles away, Rick really could plead his innocence. After all, it was his word against Len's. He could quite easily persuade Aunt Kate to give him the cottage. After all, as he lived in Toronto, he would be the one to need a getaway from the city, not his sisters who lived with bush land all about them.

Jade managed a weak sigh of relief when Len turned back. But she could not fully relax yet. Len might have seen her, or at least have known that she was in the vicinity and could be toying with her, waiting for the opportunity to pounce. He would enjoy that in a calculated way. She was sure that he would try his hardest to find her, not wanting to face Rick's hysterical tirade when her cousin found out that she had escaped. Or would he? Maybe they were not as close as they seemed. Len might be glad to be rid of Rick. While she was sitting in the tree waiting for what she felt would be a propitious time to get down, she allowed her mind to wander to Aunt Kate.

Poor Aunt Kate would be shocked to know that her only son and youngest child was a murderer. She would be disappointed to know that he was mixed up in drugs, but murder on top of that would devastate her aunt. As far as Jade knew, Aunt Kate had never done anything to hurt anyone, and Jade was sure that Kate had treated her own children as well as she had treated Jade. She wondered, not for the first time in the last few hours, what had made Rick go astray. It was less harrowing to try to analyze *his* situation than to think about *hers*.

She glanced at her watch. She had been in the tree for forty-five minutes. Her legs were cramped from her sitting perfectly still, hunched in the branches, and she was becoming chilled from the rain soaking into her clothes. Well, at least she had gotten a shower from all the rain and would be rid of the smell of vomit, she thought wryly.

Jade was certain that Len had retraced his steps to the car. She just couldn't picture him spending any more time in the rain than he absolutely had to. As it was, he would be fuming. She estimated it had taken her about twenty minutes to get as far as the pine tree, and he had covered the distance in a time equal to hers. She continued to sit in the tree for another fifteen miserable minutes before she felt it was reasonably safe to get down. As she sat there, the faint traces of light diminished even more. Unless Len had a flashlight with him, he would not take the chance of being in the bush in the dark. She climbed as quietly as she could from her high perch, then dropped to the ground. The rain-sodden moss and pine needles muted the sound of her fall to a soft whump, but the blackflies and mosquitoes targeted her in droves.

She headed in the direction of the highway through the wet undergrowth, but in a more southerly direction than where she had come in. If her reckoning was right, she should come out some distance south of Aunt Kate's place. Thinking back over the time she and Len had spent in the car, she estimated that she had entered the bush about ten kilometers south of the cottage, and if she didn't get lost, she would add about five kilometers to that distance.

Rain washed over her in chilling rivulets as she came out into more stunted growth. She pulled up short. She had been wearing a navy blue T-shirt with a rose-pink one on top. How Len had missed seeing her, she didn't know. Now, she stripped them off and replaced them in reverse order. She could not afford to make herself too visible. Her jeans were faded blue denim, and her Nikes were now so stained by mud and wet leaves that there was no white visible. Nevertheless, she began to slow down and search out the larger trees and thicker underbrush.

The birds were naturally silent in the rain. A blessing. If they had sent out warning calls at her approach, they would have been a definite giveaway. Conversely, they would also warn her of anyone else's approach, but she figured she couldn't have everything. And if she had to choose, she would choose it this way. She credited herself with having a good ear in the bush. She could pick up the sounds of snapping branches or footfalls from an extensive distance. Her ear hadn't been that great a few minutes before, though. She hadn't heard Len after her. That tree climb had been pure inspiration and good fortune.

Abruptly, she stopped. Were her powers working for her again? She fervently hoped so as she plodded onward through the sodden bush, trying to avoid the small whip-like branches. Because her left eye was now swollen completely shut, she misjudged a branch and pulled back, startled, when it punctured her cheek. More blood trickled down her wet face and she wiped it off with little thought.

One more battle scar in this warfare that was her life.

The trees thinned out, and she was brought up short by an algae-encrusted bog in front of her. Just ahead she could see the dark strip of highway. She would have to be careful, for the moment she stepped out into the open, even in the semi-darkness, she would be a target for anyone. And God only knew who was looking for her now.

She trusted nobody, except maybe Jason, but she hadn't quite made up her mind whether she trusted him or not. She thought she did, and certainly she trusted Tom. But if Jason thought she was allied with Rick, he would have the whole police force out looking for her. He had seemed to believe her when she had told him that she knew nothing about the stash of drugs, but that was before Rick and Len had shown up on the highway. Now it was anybody's guess just what part she played in the whole mess. She wasn't sure herself.

Had she just a few hours ago started to see Jason as her white knight? Well, so much for white knights. Where were they when you needed them? It seemed they came charging by only when they wanted something from you, then took off again, leaving you behind. Ignoring her throbbing head, she permitted her well-earned distrust of people to surface.

She had to make a choice, and quickly. Should she take a chance at wading through the slimy bog or should she detour around it and look for larger trees? Two factors made the decision easy--one, the certainty of snakes in the bog and two, the need for cover. Which was the more powerful reason, she couldn't have said.

Len could have spotted her quickly had she entered the bog, and waited for her to slog through the muck and mire and emerge on the other side. Or he could force her into the bog until she either fell and drowned or succumbed to exposure. That would have fitted nicely into their plans; that way she would be out of the way, and they would not be held responsible. But she hadn't come this far to fail now. She circled back through the dense brush. The tag alders and hazel bushes scratched and stabbed her. She looked at her bloody arms and felt her face tighten with a myriad of bites, scratches, welts, and punctures.

It was a good thing she wasn't overly concerned about her appearance, she reflected. If she had been, her whole perspective would have changed dramatically in the last few hours. As the stillness deepened, she crept stealthily on, stopping to listen every few moments for any sounds other than those of the bush. As she did so, she took a moment to orient herself.   The rain continued intermittently, but she trudged on for another kilometer south until she had passed the swamp and come to more solid ground.   Crouching down behind a moss-covered rock about twelve meters from the shoulder of the highway, she looked as far as she could to the north and to the south. She could not see the black Ford, nor any sign of her red car, which meant Len had probably driven down the highway to intercept her cousin as Rick scooted through the intersection of Highways Eleven and Seventeen.   Given that the visibility was low, for the moment she felt relatively safe.

She glanced at her Timex Digital and saw that it was five o'clock. It had been five hours since she had first left the cottage with Jason on her way to the safe place he had told her about. Some safe place, she scoffed softly to herself. In all honesty, however, she couldn't really fault Jason. It had been her stubborn persistence to thwart him that had landed her in this mess. She castigated herself angrily, fervently hoping the dense cloud cover would bring on an early black night. She would need all the help she could get to stay out of the clutches of the two men, but she couldn't stay behind this rock for long. What to do?

Should she chance the dash across the road? Should she stay where she was? Just why she wanted to cross the road she wasn't sure, but instinct told her that she would be safer over there. If she stayed this side, there was only one direction to go--farther south. She didn't know exactly where she was on this side of the road, anyway, but she did know it would not be safe for long. Not that it would be any different on the other side of the highway. There were no trees or rocks that she could identify, and as there were no close buildings, she had nothing by which to estimate her position. She knew she must be somewhere between Tilden Lake and Marten River. Both had a fairly large summer population, but the people would be at their scattered cottages, cabins, and camps throughout the bush. Most of them would be near small lakes or streams, not in the bush adjacent to the highway where she was now.

She decided to stay where she was for another half hour, praying the sky would get even darker. If Len had returned to his car as she suspected, he would have raced down the highway to try to catch Rick and alert him. Failing that, she could visualize him traveling by himself back to Toronto or wherever he felt safe. When he met up again with Rick, both men would be back to hunt her down. Hunger pangs gnawed at her stomach, probably because she had upchucked her only meal of the day when that rat had caressed her. Caressed? Could you call it *caressed*, when there had been no tenderness, no love involved? More like he had felt her up. Well, she had met up with all kinds of men with wandering hands before. They believed they had a prerogative to feel a woman's body whenever they felt like it. After all, they ran their hands lovingly over cars, or over stereos, why not women? None, however, had repulsed her as much as this man had. With a shudder, she glanced again at her watch.

It was now six o'clock. She had stayed longer behind the rock than she had planned, still undecided whether to chance a move or to stay. She was near exhaustion, but knew that to give in to it now would cost her life. It was fairly dark, and another rain cloud hovered nearby. Hoping it would move enough to give her more cover, she watched it for five minutes, but to no avail. It stayed hovering over the bush on the other side of the road, and she decided to take this as a good omen. Squatting down in the tall cattails just off the shoulder of the highway, and ignoring the fact that snakes liked that type of cover too, she eyed up the other side as best she could.

She would have to know precisely where she was going when she got to the other side. There was a stand of thick trees about thirty meters in from the road and slightly to the south of where she was now. She looked north and south again, then dashed across the road. Ducking across the highway, she caught a glimpse of a car just coming into her peripheral vision. She had no way of knowing who it might be, so couldn't trust that she would be rescued. She continued across, hoping that in the darkness the driver hadn't spotted her.

She skidded on a moss-covered rock and jumped over some rain-slick mud. She couldn't afford to be careless now and leave a skid mark. After all, even if Len wasn't familiar with this country, Rick was. If he came back, he would be furious. Once before today, she had seen that he had an unstable temperament and, teetering on the brink, would not hesitate to kill her. Her instinct for self-preservation was working overtime, and she felt the adrenaline surge through her body.

Without warning, the dark cloud that had been hovering let loose its burden of water, and rain poured in streams upon the bush where Jade had just entered. It seemed heavier in the spot to which she was headed. It was a mixed blessing, but Jade wasn't about to debate the issue. She scanned the trees and spotted one she thought she could climb into for protection. It was a maple, taller and more densely leaved than most of the maple trees in that area; nevertheless, it wouldn't hide her from anyone intent on finding her. But it would give her a vantage point from which to watch the highway.

With her flagging strength, she leaped up to grab onto a branch. Her hand slipped along the wet bark, chafing her skin and she fell into the mud surrounding the tree. As she was leaping up for her second try, through the rain and the darkening forest, she spotted her sports car moving slowly north along the shoulder of the road. She knew for certain now that both Len and Rick were after her. Impelled by fear, she leaped again for the branch. This time, she caught at it and pulled herself with difficulty into the tree. Panting and losing strength rapidly, she climbed and shinnied to a small branch in the uppermost part of the maple. She forced herself to hold tightly and pay attention to what she was doing. This tree was not half as safe as the one in which she had hidden on the other side of the road. She had no choice. But if she lost her concentration for even a second, she would plummet twenty feet onto the rocks and brush below.

From her vantage point above the underbrush, she could see only a part of the highway. She couldn't see her car, but was sure that Rick would drive slowly north toward the cottage. She hoped that he wouldn't even think to look for her on the east side of the highway. Len would have told him where she had gone into the bush, and both men, she was sure, would think that she was headed back toward her aunt's property. Well, that would be one place she definitely wouldn't go.

The sudden spate of rain lessened again and was now a steady pouring of minute droplets. As she continued to clutch the branch, she kept a sharp lookout. Another car sped past on its way somewhere north, its occupants unaware of the drama being played out in the country through which they were passing. Jade could imagine the conversation now. "It's boring country to travel through, isn't it, Harry?" After all, she had gone through conversations like that herself. Funny how people saw only the surface of the bush, just as they probably skimmed through the rest of life, she thought. Her nerves jumped, her reverie abruptly interrupted.

Her sports car was coming back, now traveling slowly south on the opposite side of the road. She knew they had narrowed their search, otherwise the car wouldn't have returned so quickly. Clinging stubbornly to the belief that Rick would not look for her on the east side of the road, she wondered how far down the highway he would go before he doubled back on her side. She would have to be very careful not to give any hint of her presence.

She waited, now thoroughly chilled in her sodden clothes. She had no intention of getting a chill, either. What was the good of escaping someone who tried to kill her if she just died from pneumonia or hypothermia? At least with either one, she answered herself, she could choose her own time to go, relatively speaking, of course. She wouldn't be at the whim of someone else who was bent on making her end as miserable as his life was. Why Rick should be hostile and miserable, Jade didn't know. Maybe some people were born to live miserable lives. She thought fleetingly of her parents.

Ten minutes later, the red car went past again, heading north. She didn't see the Ford, and wondered if they were both in her car, or whether Len was covering another part of the highway. Now was her time to make a move. If she could get down from the tree and farther into the bush, she would be at an advantage, because as she moved ever so slightly northward, they (if both of them were in her car) would be coming back on the opposite side of the road. That is, if they kept up the stalking for much longer. She had never been into the bush with Rick, or with any of her cousins, so she didn't know how much they knew of it. She knew only that she had spent countless hours alone here, contemplating where her life was heading and escaping from the realities of her life at home.

It had been a solitary childhood, but it had its compensations, regardless of what the psychologist had said. Like now, when she was putting her knowledge of the bush to good use. She jumped down to the ground, aware of her painful body and exhaustion. Her head throbbed from the repeated jolts and Jade felt the spurt of blood seep into her hair. Her left eye remained swollen shut.

Determined to make it farther into the bush, she plodded onward through the rain-drenched undergrowth. Even if she lost sight of Rick and Len when they continued to search along that stretch of the highway, she felt she would still have the edge. How much longer could they continue patrolling the area without being sighted by the police and stopped for questioning? Jade brightened at the thought as she stumbled through the tangled brush. She was thankful, too, that the dripping rain was keeping the masses of blackflies at bay. She knew that if she stopped once and the rain slowed to a drizzle, they would be out again. She slipped and skidded her way farther into the undergrowth, looking for a place where she could feel relatively safe curled up for the night.

If Jason thought she had gone back to Toronto, he would not try to look for her here. He might even have returned to Toronto himself. No one would know that she was here except for Rick and Len, the two people she would rather didn't know.

She trudged on, vaguely recognizing that her fatigue was causing her to make mistakes and to stumble more frequently. Where were her favorite author's miraculous people now? Jon Land's characters seemed able to keep up indefinitely. She had often wondered how they could be shot in Beirut and a few hours later board a plane to the United States or vice versa. Where did they get their stamina? Or did that come under the heading of "the suspension of disbelief" so important to the creative writer.

She couldn't marshal her thoughts; her resources were spent, and her mind was already starting to dwell in the realm of her delirium, just a small twist of the mind away from the part that controlled her visions. Where were all the good characters of all the mystery and spy novelists when she needed them? Where were all her white knights when she was in distress? A picture of them all together at a party, talking about their good deeds and miraculous rescues, floated through her befuddled mind. She tittered at the mind picture. She felt hot and the sight in her one good eye became blurred, but at least the rain was mitigating her thirst.

A large grey granite rock caught her attention. On the east side of the rock, away from the highway and partly hidden by wild bramble bushes, was a small hollow. She tried to think logically, to go over the pros and cons of staying in the shelter for a short time. After a few moments, she conceded defeat. Her mind was not working logically or rationally. She rubbed her foot over the moss and looked carefully for anything else that might be using the small cave for shelter.

As the overhang faced away from the pelting rain, the hollow was dry. The water that dripped continuously over the overhang of the rock caused a misty curtain to form over the small opening. She let out a long sigh and, looking askance at her sodden clothing, curled herself into a ball to give herself whatever warmth she could muster. Before long she was dozing in a semi-delirium, but lucid enough to recognize that she had to be extremely quiet. She couldn't afford to have Rick and his accomplice discover her through any slip-up that she might make. Smiling to herself and wondering whether she was beginning to think like a criminal or an animal, she shivered to bring warmth to her deadened limbs, and fell into an uneasy sleep.

CHAPTER SIX

Racing up the highway after he left District Twelve, Jason reflected on his telephone conversation with Tom. Tom had exploded when he heard that Jade was with her cousin.

"Jay, how could you let her go with them?"

He could hear Tom pacing back and forth for the length of the telephone cord.

"I'm kicking myself, too, but I couldn't very well have prevented her from going without giving a good reason. And I didn't want to give them any more information than necessary."

She had seemed happy to see her cousin at first, Jason explained. If she had known that Rick was involved in selling drugs, she would have appeared at least anxious when they had driven up, more so if she had been involved. Thinking back to when her cousin and his friend had arrived at the location where Jason had the flat tire, he found the image of Jade's face hovering in his memory. She had an open face that showed her every emotion, and there was clearly something about her cousin that had unnerved her.

He was more upset than he had been in years and felt the need for his grandmother's wise counsel. How could he approach her and not cast his burdens upon her aging shoulders? He was not a rebellious teen anymore. His Ojibway grandmother had always cared deeply for him, which was why he felt closer to his Ojibway heritage than to his Scots one.

His Scottish grandparents he had seen only twice--once when they had visited Canada, and once when he had visited them in Scotland. It was through no fault of theirs that they had not been closer. Distance had proved to be an effective barrier, and when his parents had been killed and he had been taken in by his Ojibway grandparents, he had lost contact with the Scottish side of his family entirely, until his visit to them when he was older. Now they, too, had passed on.

He wondered if both sets of ancestors accounted for his "hunches." Both ethnic groups were known to have so-called far-seeing powers, like he suspected Jade possessed. He considered himself normal--if there was such a thing as normal.

When he left North Bay, he had not yet made up his mind whether he would stop at Jade's cottage or continue to his grandmother's, but as he reached the turn-off to Jade's cottage, the car seemed to turn into her drive automatically.

He hoped that Jade and the two men were still there--maybe even having a good time; then his mind could be set at ease. Even as he thought this, he had a strong premonition. He brought the car to an abrupt halt and swung himself out at the same time. The only car in evidence was an unmarked Crown Victoria. The same officer was on duty and came over to meet him. "Where is everyone?" Jason demanded of the man.

"They left about three hours ago," explained the young officer, looking at his watch.

Jason checked his, too. It was 4:45. He had left Jade at noon.

"I called Tom only about half an hour ago because something didn't seem right, but I couldn't put my finger on anything definite," the officer said. He looked discomfitted, wondering if he should say what was on his mind. Jason saw fine beads of perspiration on the younger man's brow. The poor guy. First Jason with the girl; then blurting out about the surveillance; then having three supposed suspects take off. Jason was glad he wasn't in his shoes, but he said nothing. "They came back with the girl shortly after you left with her, and went into the cottage. They were there for about an hour, then they left. They said they were going back to Toronto.

"The dark guy with the glasses took the girl with him in his car, and the blond guy took the girl's red sports car." The officer checked his notations in his black book. "The guy driving the sports car sped out of here and left the Ford to follow. Something's not right," the officer emphasized again. "I would have called earlier, but the girl didn't seem to mind going. Everything appeared normal, but it isn't, I know."

So, Jason's mind kept spinning. Jade had left with Len. Why? And were they really heading for Toronto? He doubted it. Jason felt a wave of sympathy for the young cop. He remembered what it was like to be a young officer and have suspicions that you couldn't explain. If the guy had told anyone else about his doubts, he would have been the butt of the good-natured kidding that took place in every squad. Yet, Jason knew that it was gut instinct that more often than not solved a case. The young officer, who stood before him sweating and not a little embarrassed, went up in Jason's estimation.

"But you did call Tom?" he verified, thinking that it must have been just after he, himself, had talked to Tom.

The officer nodded.

"Good going!" Jason commended him. "I'll just check the cottage and then I'll carry on to my grandmother's cottage on Highway 64. She has a telephone, but I don't want to be contacted there unless it is absolutely an emergency. If you have anything else to report, phone North Bay. If you can get Tom, talk to him, or you may call him at his home number. Do you have it?" Jason had no compunction about having the officer disturb Tom at home.

The officer nodded. "But I should be going off shift. I'm just waiting for my replacement." He had regretted his earlier brashness in offering to help the detective with the girl. No one who was taking advantage of a girl would be this worried about her. This guy really cared. He stammered, "About what I said earlier . . ."

"Forget it," Jason interrupted him. "I know what you thought. And you were right to be concerned."

The officer swallowed. "I just want to say I'm sorry. I thought I had been told that she was under surveillance. I gather you didn't think so."

"No," Jason returned. "I didn't. But it wouldn't have made any difference."

Nodding his understanding, the officer was about to say that he knew that Jason cared about the girl, but something held him back. Then he determined what it was. Jason, himself, didn't realize just how deeply his caring went.

He gave Jason an enigmatic smile that reminded the detective of Tom's earlier observation. Jason frowned at him as he opened the door to the cottage.

As far as Jason could see, nothing had changed. The only thing missing was Jade's suitcase. Even so, he suspected that the two men had coerced her into going with them. Were they returning to Toronto? He didn't think Jade would be willing to go back just yet, regardless of the fact that her holiday to this point had been anything but what she had expected it to be.

After he had discovered Jade unconscious on the floor of the small room, he and Tom had searched the cottage thoroughly and come up with several kilos of cocaine and packets of marijuana, obviously hidden there by someone who hoped to market it. He suspected the man in the dark Ford car, but now knew with a certainty that even Toronto didn't have that the cousin was involved more deeply than anyone had thought. Where the smaller, older man fit in, he wasn't sure. He shut the cottage door and beckoned to the officer. "Could you stay for the next shift? I wouldn't normally ask anyone to do a double shift, but I want as few people as possible in on this. If you don't mind staying, I'll clear it with your boss."

Having secured the young officer's okay, Jason drove away to the cottage where he knew he would be welcomed. Reluctantly, he used the car phone to call the North Bay headquarters.

"I'm glad you called in," the duty sergeant said urgently. "You're supposed to contact the Toronto office again."

"They didn't tell you what they wanted?"

"Probably didn't want too many people to know, and after all, they probably think we're not used to dealing with big time stuff here. Likely look on us as hicks." His voice held lightly-veiled resentment.

Jason didn't tell him that what he said was true. Even in the police force, petty jealousies and rivalries were rife in the organization.   The city cops did think they were superior. Jason, however, had known both sides, and knew the advantages to be gained in one of the smaller areas, especially if you had a young family, such as Tom had. He pulled into a Husky service station-restaurant and placed a call to Toronto. After what seemed an interminable wait, he was connected with someone who felt he should be given more information.

"It's good of you to feel that way," Jason informed him sarcastically. But what Toronto told him sent chills down his back and turned his stomach to water. He talked for a few minutes and hung up. Looking at his watch, he dialed Tom's home at Tilden Lake. Tom would have just returned home from work and was probably looking forward to a few minutes alone with his wife and kids. Jason had only a minute touch of sympathy for him.

When Tom answered, his voice was heavy with fatigue. But at the moment, Jason felt his own need was greater, and knew that Tom's annoyance would abate after he heard Jason's news. Jason didn't bother with civilities but dived right in the second Tom picked up the phone.

"You know that Derek guy, the guy Jade was mixed up with in Toronto?" he asked Tom.

"Yeah," Tom affirmed, now alerted by Jason's abrupt tone.

"He's undercover," Jason told him. "He's a Narc. Apparently quite good. They had to go through with the questioning of Jade to keep his cover secure. As far as the underworld knows, and as far as anyone else knows, they let Jade go because of insufficient evidence. According to the guy I talked to, though, they still think she might have some drug connection to her cousin."

Tom whistled over the telephone, causing Jason to pull away sharply from the receiver. "Does Jade know about any of this?"

"I don't think so. This Derek kept up the relationship with Jade hoping they could catch her getting in touch with the cousin." Jason was about to add more, with some profanity thrown in for good measure, but quelled the urge. He continued: "They're pretty sure of the cousin's involvement now, as they've had a positive ID from an informant. Tom, Jade is with them now," Jason's anguished voice continued. "Or at least with Len." An image of Jade alone with either one of the men knotted Jason's stomach. Which of the two was worse?

"Where would they go?" Tom's voice was full of concern.

"I don't know. According to Officer Bentley, they said they were returning to Toronto. Jade went with the older guy, Len, in the Ford, and the cousin took Jade's car. But I don't believe they've left the area yet. I just feel it."

"Jay, I'm going to pull the car off surveillance duty. To

hell with Toronto. Come down to our house and leave your car, then we'll go on from there. Okay?" Tom's voice exuded the professional calm that Jason knew he himself was losing.

Without giving it much thought, he agreed to Tom's suggestion. He knew what Tom's strategy was. With the surveillance car out of the way, there was just the off-chance that the two men would return to the cottage, thinking it completely safe.

While he waited for Jason to arrive, Tom released a bulletin to all detachments south to Toronto to keep a lookout for both the dark Ford and the red sports car, with orders to detain both drivers on suspected possession with intent to traffic. That would hold both men for a short time anyway.

When Jason arrived, he had Tom send the message to the units north of Marten River and west to Sudbury and Espanola, just in case the men tried to circumvent the southern area and head north or west instead. He doubted they were intelligent enough to think the situation through to that point--at least Len wasn't. Rick seemed capable of forethought, but was in all likelihood on the edge of panic.

His assessment of Rick's personality was the same as Jade's. If the two men believed that they were under suspicion and being watched, they could take an alternate route down Highway 169 or even down the old Highway 11, or a number of secondary routes, including through Manitoulin Island where they could access the ferry over to Tobermory. From there, they could drive down Highway 21, along Lake Huron to Highway 401 and return to Toronto from the west.

If they had indeed left for Toronto, Jason didn't think they would get that far without being seen by somebody somewhere. But it was now tourist season, so there were a great many more cars on the highways. The red sports car would not be all that hard to detect, but the dark Ford

Fiesta would blend in with many more like it. And he could bet that Jade was not in her sports car if she had been forced into going along with them.

By the time he had reached Tom's house, Jason had formed a plan. "I'm going back to the cottage," he told Tom. "Can you have someone drive me, so I won't have to take my car? I don't want anyone to know I'm there." He was hoping that neither of the two men was near the cottage yet, but had a hunch that one or the other would return--with or without Jade. He hadn't seen anyone on his way to Tom's, but if the intent of the two men was to hole up in the cottage for a while, thinking they would be safe there, they could well have hidden their tracks and entered the cottage from the dense bush at the back.

When he had passed Jade's cottage on the way to Tom's, the unmarked car had already gone, and he had been tempted to stop in. But he knew that he wouldn't have gotten as far as the door without being seen, and he was counting on the element of surprise. Tom now agreed with Jason's plan and suggested that they both go.

"No." Jason was adamant. "If you like, you can be on the alert, but I don't want any cars or anyone to be seen around the cottage." He didn't add that he hoped to get to them first, but gave Tom a look which the other man interpreted correctly.

"Jason, just remember, you're a good cop. Don't do anything stupid. Let the system do its job."

"The damn system has so far allowed these two guys to be on the streets and has used an innocent person. Where's the justice in that?"

"Jason . . . ."

Jason nodded, checked out his firearm, and put on his shoulder holster. He hadn't worn it when he had been with Jade. His wife hadn't like guns, and he assumed Jade wouldn't either. His wayward thoughts insisted on comparing the two women. Why? From what he had seen so far, they were nothing alike. Jade was independent. His wife had been the dependent type. He was sure that Jade would be able to get along fine without him.

His wife had wanted him by her side all the time. Even when she shopped for groceries or clothes, she had needed him there beside her, asking his opinion, conceding to his views on everything from cereal to suits, from fruit to frying pans. He hadn't realized it at the time. The image had only now occurred to him. He didn't really like the idea of Jade's getting along without him, but that was another matter. He didn't even know what he wanted anymore, except that he wanted Jade, and he liked the idea of that.

Lorraine spoke up for the first time after greeting Jason. "Stay for supper, Jason. You look exhausted. And Tom should eat too," she coaxed. A look of understanding passed between Tom and his wife, but Jason merely looked at her numbly. The very thought of food on his tensed-up stomach nauseated him.

"Lorraine, honey, after being married to a police officer for eighteen years, you should know that when we're on a case, that's where our whole attention is."

Looking exclusively at her husband, Lorraine spoke softly: "*My* whole attention is on keeping my husband alive and well." Tom lifted his shoulder in a slight shrug and kissed her cheek as Jason hurried to the car.

They rode to Jade's cottage with only a few snatches of desultory conversation. Jason was engrossed in comparing the two women in his life, past and present, and in schooling himself to be the professional that he had been up to now. As they neared their destination, he focused his mind.

"Let me out on the highway north of the cottage. That way, I can approach it from the bush at the north end." He was about to order Tom to return to his home and keep out of any trouble that might ensue, then realized that the order would be neither fair nor professional. And besides, Tom wouldn't follow it anyway. His friend wasn't about to let him down now. Even if Tom hadn't been intent on solving the murder, he would have stayed with Jason.

He let Jason out in a small turn-off, keeping the passenger door hidden from the road. When Jason was well into the cover of the trees, Tom turned off the engine and continued to sit, holding a pad in front of him. He had planned his cover before Jason had reached his home. Any curious eyes would note the radar apparatus on the dash and assume a speed check was in process.

Stealthily, Jason moved through the wet undergrowth until he was close enough to get a good view of the cottage and the surrounding grounds. Mindful of the dampness of his clothes as he went through the bush, he was thankful that he had cut the tall grass and weeds surrounding the cottage. It was not only less wet, but it afforded him an unobstructed view. There was no sign of a car or of anyone on foot, but Jason knew that didn't mean anything. If the two men were intent on hiding, they could do it quite well in this area of isolated bush.

Tom had a cell phone with him, and Jason felt sure that if serious trouble erupted, Tom would be under cover close by and have back-up in no time. He would have issued orders to the unmarked to stay available and out of sight. Nevertheless, Jason was more or less on his own. He could either get killed or kill the two men before any help arrived. The thought of this and of how quickly a life could be snuffed out caused a murderous rage to surge through him as he thought of Rick's strong-arm tactics with Jade.

If there was anything that could have made him recognize the situation from a more positive perspective, then that image was it. He had no intention of losing his life for any reason, now that he felt he was just beginning to live again. The scent of damp earth and wet leaves calmed him.

Creeping to the window he had only recently replaced, he didn't try to reason why he had left it unlocked when he had brought Jade back from Tom's house earlier. He was glad that some sort of intuition had been at work, because he needed that window to open silently. He didn't want to chance trying the front door in case anyone was watching. He wished he hadn't stayed so long in North Bay. It was now dark, and the insidious rain began again, pelting him with icy drops as he quickly and quietly pried open the window and hauled his wet body over the sill.

Years of sitting at a desk hadn't done him any favors in the muscle development area. If he had been in great physical shape before, he sure wasn't now. He lay for a moment panting in the darkness. The interior had lost its former comforting atmosphere. He sniffed. Sweat. The room was filled with the odor of fear and loathing.

He reproached himself for not having been on the lookout earlier. But, logically, with the little information he had previously had at his disposal there was nothing he could have done. He now suspected that the homicide of the young girl was in some way, indeed, tied in with Jade, and if the girl had been killed by someone thinking that they were killing Jade, then Jade's life at this moment was in jeopardy. As of that moment, however, Jason felt certain that she was alive. If she were already dead, he would have felt the aloneness in his soul.

In her shallow cave, Jade mumbled and thrashed about in her delirium. Ghostly snakes were crawling over her and she tried to brush them off. How long she had lain there she didn't know, nor at this point did she care. She thought she saw a bright light, and in that light stood a tall, handsome Indian. His gleaming blue-black hair was pulled back from his face in a ponytail. Jade's fogged mind registered that his face was unlined and shone with an inner peace. Despite his high-bridged nose giving him an aristocratic expression, there was a softness about him that negated any haughtiness he might portray. He wore a fringed deerskin jacket, which she could tell had been lovingly worked with porcupine quills and beads. His leggings were of soft-worked deerskin, and hand-made deerskin moccasins covered his feet.

"Jade!" he whispered softly, looking at her battered and swollen face. "You cannot stay here. You will join the spirit world if you do, and your time has not come yet. If you enter too soon, you will have to bide your time in the realm of confusion, neither here nor there. You must stir yourself, *noozhishe,* and follow me. We have many steps to travel before you are safe." He put out a warm hand and stroked her swollen face. Blood covered her scalp from her opened wound. She was burning with fever, but her exhausted body clung precariously and tenaciously to life, obeying her strength of spirit as far as it was able.

Jade stirred and murmured. What did he mean she couldn't stay here? She didn't want to move. She was hot and her throat felt burned and raw. Her head pounded unceasingly every time she moved an inch. She seemed to have a lot of headaches lately. She put a hand up to her aching head. First one thing and then another.

Frowning in bewilderment, she looked at the man before her. He looked not much older than Jade herself, or possibly Jason. The thought of Jason raised her temperature even more. Even in her fevered state she noticed a resemblance between Jason and the man who was bending over her with a tender smile. Because of that resemblance, she was not afraid of the man before her. "Who are you?"

He smiled. "My name will mean nothing to you yet. You will find out soon. *Ambe, noozhishe.* Come, my grandchild." He held out a hand to help her up. "Soon you will meet your destiny."

She was reluctant to leave her warm bed, destiny or no destiny, but knew through some inner knowledge that she must force herself to stand up, to get her circulation going. Unquestioningly, she reached for the Indian's extended hand. He helped her to her feet, then without another word, turned and walked away. She followed her guide into the bush, too feverish to do much rational thinking, and not noticing that he was leading her in a northerly direction. He was silent and seemed to glide through the underbrush with little trouble, whereas she was having a much more difficult time of it, stumbling over roots and stubbing her toes on small rocks.

Her jeans were still sodden, and as she moved, the chilled fabric chafed her hot flesh. The rain had lessened but the sky was dark. Jade had no idea of the time. She had no idea what day it was either. For all she knew she could have been in the bush for hours or days or weeks. Beyond thought or caring, she knew only that she hovered between two worlds and that it was her decision which one she chose.

She was unaware that Rick and Len were still searching for her along the highway. They had decided to try twice more before heading back to the cottage, anticipating that she would return there. Rick, not knowing Jade well at all, thought she would go back to her comfortable bolt hole. Where else would she feel as safe?. They decided to look along the shoulders of the highway for another hour. If they could get her before she got to her aunt's cottage, they could get out of the area before anyone became suspicious and tried to stop them.

The Indian beckoned for her to keep close to him. They had to go around a mosquito-infested swamp, which meant either that they had to go farther east into the bush or closer to the highway. Regardless of the route he chose, they had several hours of traveling. He doubted that Jade would be able to keep up the pace if they went deeper into the bush. To go nearer to the highway would bring her closer to her adversaries, but would offer more solid terrain for walking.

He chose the route closer to the highway. Even so, the going was difficult for her. The undergrowth was dense with tag alders and wild hazel bushes. Although to Jade he appeared to walk through the branches oblivious to their existence, he invariably held the branches so they would not snap back in her face. She stumbled on in a daze.

At one point he put out a hand to steady her as she seemed about to slip away from consciousness. She slid on the wet mossy stones, and scraped her already swollen face against the rough bark of a tree that she hadn't even noticed. She wanted to talk to him, to find out who he was, but she couldn't find the energy. It took all the strength she possessed and every ounce of willpower just to keep tramping and slipping and sliding and falling to wherever it was he was leading her. Her soul cried out for Jason.

The Indian guide turned to her with an assured and piercing look. "He will come, my granddaughter. Be patient." She hadn't thought that she had spoken aloud, but perhaps she had. When they came close to the highway, she was disconcerted to see the black Ford traveling slowly along the shoulder in the same direction. The Indian put his finger to his lips and held her arm as he pulled her behind a rock out of sight of the road. The car stopped. Both Len and Rick stepped out onto the shoulder and scanned the sparser bush where she and the Indian now stood, concealed from their view.

"There are those," the Indian spoke quietly, "who choose to meet most of their problems early in life. There are those who choose to meet them frequently throughout their journey in the earth realm, and there are those who choose to live well at the beginning and meet their problems later in life. You have chosen to meet yours early.

That is the choice of the wise soul." He smiled. "Come, we must be on our way; the two men have left this side of the road."

As he maneuvered her again through the dense growth, she ruminated over what he had said. Or what she thought he had said. She wasn't even sure he had spoken. Now that the rain had stopped, the battalions of blackflies and mosquitoes returned to their crusade. For the first part of the trek, she had swatted at them furiously, but even that extra movement had sapped what little strength she had. Now she just let them bite and probe her. She visualized her remaining life force being sucked up into their bodies so they could produce their own offspring. Survival of the fittest. She would never get the chance have a child of her own. But if she would not be able to reproduce, then why should they? She hoped that her blood would transmit a virus to them; then they would be killed off. *Fever do your thing. Fever do your thing. Fever do your thing.* The refrain became a mantra from which she drew strength.

She trudged on into the darkness, now deepening rapidly. The Indian seemed to know his way quite well, and even though Jade was having difficulty seeing and even more difficulty staying on her feet, she felt that she could make it to wherever they were going as long as she focused on the mysterious man who trod a few steps ahead of her. She hadn't known the natives still wore deerskin clothing. Was it superior to the synthetics she was used to?

She experienced no apprehension with the Indian, only the profound dependence and trust she had found with Jason. When she noticed a snake, scarcely more black than the blackness about them, for the first time in her life she felt no fear of the reptile. They left the highway and headed in an easterly direction again. This was taking more time, but safety was the prime consideration for the Indian.

Now he turned again and led her farther north. Jade

had no idea where they were. She had never been this far into the bush on this side of the highway. She knew that there were cabins and cottages scattered throughout the area, but so far they had come upon no habitation whatsoever.

Even through her fever, she wondered vaguely why she wasn't more suspicious of this man who was guiding her. After all, she knew nothing about him, and for all she knew he could have been working with her cousin. Her slight doubt did not materialize into anything greater. The man had the gentleness of spirit that she had found in Jason, not the harsh hostility that exuded from both Rick and Len.

As he led her once more close to the highway, they again saw the black Ford. This time it was retracing its route on the opposite side of the road. She was thankful that they were now going in opposite directions. Her gratefulness was short-lived, however, when the car made a U-turn in the middle of the highway and circled back north in the direction Jade and the Indian were traveling.

The Indian frowned. He didn't want the girl to know, but there was really no need for the men to be looking this far north of her cottage, unless they had some knowledge that she would be heading in this direction. He pulled Jade to a halt behind a pine tree as he silently analyzed their situation. His stoic features showed no sign of his thoughts. After several moments he turned back to her and gently pushed her shoulder to guide her farther along their route.

It seemed like days since he had pulled her up out of her warm cave under the rock overhang. The hard trudge through the bush served to heighten her fever even more. Finally, they came again to the highway, and the Indian crept closer to the pavement to search for the car.

He could see nothing. His eyesight, he knew, was far superior to that of the two men now looking for Jade. He beckoned her. She was totally exhausted. He knew that in her delirium and fever she was relying on survival instincts to keep her going. She was one tough lady, and he reminded himself to tell Grandmother that.   For a descendent of a white European, she had a lot of spunk.

Jason sat in a wooden straight-backed chair in a darkened corner of the kitchen alcove, going over and over again all the fragments of information he had gathered from various sources. The drug involvement in Toronto was the key, of course. He was glad that this Derek guy was a cop. Jade seemed to gravitate toward whatever it was that exuded from law enforcement officers. She didn't go for the criminal element. Then again, maybe they were not all that much different, the criminal element and the law enforcement officers.   He had seen it many times. Some characteristics of the two were the same. Yet, one chose to be law abiding and one chose to flout the law. He could feel himself tensing up again. This wasn't good. To pass the time and keep his mind off Jade, he speculated on the similarities and differences between the two elements: the law breaker and the law enforcer.   What made one person go one way, and the other person go another route? The old nature versus nurture question again. Who could say how a child would react to something that could be totally innocent?   Grandma had said, *"Bless your heart Jason. That was thoughtful of you to help me weed the garden."* Later, one of his younger cousins had approached him, "Jason, how come Grandma never blesses my heart?"

He glanced at his watch. It was ten o'clock, and pitch-black because of the overcast skies. As he sat mulling over the new-found information that he had received from Toronto, there was a   scuffling sound at the replaced window, and a rush of adrenalin coursed through him.   It was where he had expected them to enter. They couldn't take the chance of coming in through the front door, although the cottage was partially hidden from the highway and was barely discernable in the darkness. He hadn't heard a car drive up, so assumed they had left the cars hidden somewhere along the highway. Their thinking was the same as his. That was a frightening thought.

He waited, sinking back farther into the shadows of the dark room. He itched to get at both of them and hoped they had returned together. His hand went to his gun. Rick was the first to crawl in through the window, followed by Len. Neither man saw Jason at first, but as the cottage was small, it did not take them long to notice him sitting in the darkness with his gun pulled on them. They both drew up short, Rick reaching for his gun.

"I wouldn't do that." Jason's deep voice was quiet. His hand was trembling and he had to force himself to calm down. It had been a long time since he had pulled a gun on anyone, and at the moment he wanted to kill these guys more than anything else he had ever wanted. It took tremendous self-control not to pull the trigger, and he informed them of that through clenched teeth. "And what have you put Jade through? Where is she?"

Rick snorted. "What have we put her through? Is this the pot calling the kettle black?" he mocked. Jason gave him marks for chutzpah. The guy never knew when to quit.

"Seems to me you cops have put her through a lot more than we have." He spoke as if he knew all that had gone on, Jason observed. Jade wouldn't have told them. This meant Rick was close to the drug scene in Toronto; otherwise, he wouldn't have known about Jade's interrogation.

Jason refused to be drawn in by Rick's accusation. "Where is she?" he growled, almost losing it.

"We don't know." Both men spoke at once.

Len added, "She ran off into the bush."

"Why?" Jason spoke in a deceptively soft voice. "Why would she run off into the bush, I wonder?" When neither of the two men said anything, he continued to prod them, waving his gun menacingly. "Did she feel safer in the bush than with you?"

"We were just taking her back to Toronto," Rick spoke out, defensively. "She was riding with Len. When she ran off he tried to find her, and when he couldn't, he caught up with me on the highway, so we both came back. You know how mixed up she is." He didn't have to add that they were both looking for her so they could kill her. She had guessed too much and learned too much about them. Jason had already come to that conclusion on his own.

The hours of waiting in the cottage had provided him with the answer. He had sat in the dark piecing all the information together. He watched Rick and Len. Rick looked from Jason to Len. Len was now regarding Rick with less than his usual admiration. Len seemed to be assessing Rick, questioning his loyalty to him. By his expression, Jason knew he had come to an unfavorable conclusion. Jason, himself, could see that Rick was unstable. And he was sure that Len was too, but of the two men, Len seemed to be mentally and emotionally stronger. Jason kept silent. Divide and conquer.

Now, Jason could see Rick sizing him up, deciding whether or not killing him was a viable option. Cop killer would be added to the list of crimes already against him. Was it worth it? Rick had expected Len to back him up, but with the other man's cool regard of him, Rick knew he would be on his own.

Jason looked at Len, who seemed less and less enthusiastic about their situation. To Len, what had started out as a little drug trafficking on the side had quickly escalated out of control. He hadn't realized what a tenuous hold Rick had on the reality of situations. Rick seemed to live from one outburst to the next. Len wasn't sure if it was worthwhile siding with Rick. The killing of the girl was proof of that. Who would get the blame? Len was sure it wouldn't be Rick. He decided to take control of the situation.

"Tell you what, Cop. How be you and me cut a little deal." Len's whining voice coaxed Jason. He caught Jason's eye and couldn't miss the cynicism and disgust there. He would not fare well in Jason's hands. But then, after his attempt at bargaining, he wouldn't last long with Rick either. He glanced at Rick now. He remembered Rick's assessing look when he found out that Len had raped the other girl before he killed her. Of course, raping her had been his own idea. Just a little fun. Hell, a guy had to get some fun out of life. Len had told Rick how much he had enjoyed the experience, the rushing high he had felt knowing he was going to kill her as soon as he had finished with her.

Jason could see that Rick was reaching the point where any little remark could throw him off balance. Sizing up the characters of the two men, Jason snapped, "Where is she?" He could not picture Jade in the bush alone. She had not recovered yet from the head wound that the punk in front of him had inflicted. It had been raining all day, and she would have been running like a fugitive.

It dawned on Jason that was exactly what Jade felt she was. She was running from both the criminals who wanted her dead and from the law who wouldn't shed many tears if she happened to die. As far as she knew, she was a suspect in drug trafficking, and she wasn't far wrong in her thinking. She had no idea who Derek really was. To her he was a dealer and she was of doubtful character as far as the police were concerned.

"Rick left her with me so I could have . . ." Len said suddenly, without thinking.

Rick swung around to face him. "Shut up, you crazy bastard!" Rick's voice had taken on a high-pitched tone. He was nearing the edge. Jason stood with an appearance of calm, waiting for the moment when everything would come together and he would know he had the upper hand. Suddenly, Rick lashed out, flailing both arms, first at Len who took the full brunt of his fists across his face, then at Jason, who grabbed Rick's arms and forced them behind his back, holding them with one of his own, as he held his gun steadily on Len.

Judging that Jason would shoot as a last resort, regardless of how upset he was, Len decided to try for his escape, and pulled the trigger of his previously hidden small gun just as Tom and two officers burst through the door, guns drawn. In the ensuing melee and the darkness, Len streaked through the open window and escaped through a path that he and Rick had made through the dense brush.

CHAPTER SEVEN

"Thank . . . God . . . you got . . . here," Jason panted. Blood dripped from his head and ran down his face. The bullet from Len's gun had cut a swath from above his right temple to the middle of his scalp. As he helped to handcuff Rick, he frowned over his obvious lack of physical fitness. He had been away from this type of work for too long. He inhaled deeply, ignoring the cramping pain.

"The other one just went out the window; I'm going after him." His voice sounded harsh even to his ears.

"No." Tom detained him with a firm hand on his arm, then went to supervise the arrest. They placed Rick in the police cruiser, securely installed behind the wire mesh screen. An officer stood at the door on the driver's side, keeping an eye on the prisoner while Tom took Jason aside and looked at his head wound.

"It's superficial, but you'd better have it looked at. Come with me. The two constables can get this guy back to North Bay. You and I'll visit Emergency first. No, Jason," he added, as Jason started to argue. "You're in no shape to go after him. We'll look for him tomorrow with the K-9 unit." Tom gave further instructions to the two police officers, then seated himself in his car beside a Jason who had aged ten years in the last few hours.

Jason dropped his anguished face in his hands. "I came this close to shooting the bastards," he muttered, holding his thumb and forefinger a scant eighth-inch apart. "Tom, I'm losing it. This isn't the way I work."

Tom's eyes glinted with humor, tinged with sympathy. "For starters, my friend, you didn't shoot them. You had yourself under more control than you think. You're an excellent cop, Jay. The whole department acknowledges that. Hey, why do you think you've done so well in Toronto? It can't be your scintillating personality; you haven't been the best of company for the past few years, you know. I'm happy to see you've toppled from that pedestal. It must've been pretty cold there some nights."

"It was," Jason acknowledged the observation and knew that he had to say no more. He and Tom understood each other perfectly.

"You've joined the human race, my friend. Whether you know it or not, you love that girl. Don't tell me you just met her four days ago. It doesn't matter, you know. Love doesn't operate on a time schedule. Hell, Lorraine and I knew we were meant for each other the first time we met, and I'll tell you a secret. That's the best love there is."

Jason looked at him quizzically. "What do you mean, the best love there is? Love is love."

"Is it?" Tom asked him. "You loved Marty when you married her, didn't you?"

Jason nodded.

"But I'll bet," Tom continued, "that it wasn't the same as what you're feeling for Jade now. There are all kinds of love and many degrees of love. And what you have for Jade is one of the greatest. 'Nuff said, old friend, we had better get back with this guy and get you to the hospital."

"Where is she, Tom?" Jason whispered. "I can't bear to know that Len's out in the bush when she's there."

"I don't know, but I'll tell you this. Wherever she is, she's okay. I never thought I would say this, but go see your grandmother, if you haven't already. She always seems to have a way of finding out things, and we'll get a full scale search on for Jade, and for Rick's accomplice."

Jason shook his head as he followed Tom through the

door of the hospital. He wasn't worried about his wound. He didn't even feel it. Finding Jade was more important. What were her thinking processes? Which way would she go? He couldn't begin to think the way she did, but he didn't want her found by the police tracking dog. It would be the ultimate humiliation for her. And, although he said nothing to Tom, he felt that a full scale search, even if it were only for Len, would send Jade deeper into hiding from all of them.

He had to start his search as soon as possible, for the rain hadn't let up all day, and even in the bush Jade would have been drenched, especially if she felt she had to keep on the move ahead of the two men looking for her. Although he felt sure she was alive at the moment, he knew she could soon die from exposure, if not from Len. Perseverance was an innate part of who she was, but if she was drenched and had lost her body heat, hypothermia would set in, and she would drift into fatal sleep. He had to find her before that happened. His grandmother's spirit world would have to wait for her because he wanted his chance first. He said as much to Tom, who grinned.

Jason left the hospital and returned to the OPP detachment to fill out the necessary forms. He was in a hurry to get back to Marten River. Tom and he flew over the road to Tilden Lake to pick up Jason's car. Jason leaned back against the seat, mulling over all the possible ways that he could look for Jade without frightening her more than she was already. The two criminals had come to the cottage in the black Ford, so Jason didn't know where her red sports car was. "Tom, try to get Rick to tell you the whereabouts of Jade's car, will you?" Rick would be held in North Bay unless Toronto had a particular reason for wanting him immediately. It was past midnight, but Jason's anxiety level kept any thoughts of sleep at bay.

Rick would have taken the car off the road somewhere and hidden it in the bush. The man wasn't so stupid that he didn't know it would be conspicuous just about anywhere. That was one of the reasons Jason had been able to stop Jade in the first place. He had thought she was some wild kid out for a joy ride, unaware that when he signaled for her to bring her car to a halt, his action would cause him agony, frustration, guilt--and a growing sense of fulfillment.

The Indian led Jade across the highway safely, and they were now close to the secondary highway leading to Field and Sturgeon Falls. It was a beautiful region, filled with his people's memories and history. The images surrounded him, enclosing him in their warmth. He knew Rick had gone this way earlier, ignorant that hidden in the trees was the cottage at which Jade would be safe.

Just as they entered the bush on the opposite side, his acute hearing picked up the sounds of another human being, a man who was a shell, without heart or soul. The Indian could feel the emptiness of him, the blackness, a receptacle for evil. He wanted to escape the clutches of the man's miserable emptiness. The girl, who walked just slightly behind him, was about to lose consciousness, her resources sapped beyond any limits she had ever encountered before. If she lost control of her mind, the man's evil purposes could be carried out, for he would be able to enter her without a struggle--unless the spirit world intervened. There was only one problem--a big one.

In the earthly realm it was difficult for the spirits to maintain their great strength for any length of time. He paused only briefly before deciding to ignore the person and take Jade quietly at an angle away from him. It would be better for the police to confront and apprehend the man. They were not exhausted, not vulnerable as the girl was.

The two came at last to a small brook, and the Indian lifted her effortlessly across. They were in a beautiful glade. Even in her fever and delirium, Jade recognized it as the glade of her visions. It was close to midnight, but the place was filled with an ethereal glow, brighter than sunlight. She was rational enough to admonish herself. The light had to be moonlight. She overlooked the fact that up till that point the moon's light had been obscured by the dense cloud cover.

The cottage of her vision unfolded before her. The Indian led her to the open door in which stood a smiling Native woman. She was aged and wrinkled, but her face spoke of years of love. She held out her arms to Jade.

"Come, my child. I've been waiting for you." She took Jade inside and smiled at the young Indian who had led the girl through the bush. "Thank-you." She spoke simply. "Must you go just yet? I have need of you, Old One."

Jade was more confused than ever. The woman had called the young Indian *Old One*, yet it was the woman who was old, probably old enough to be the young man's grandmother.

He smiled at her and then at Jade. "I will stay for a short while, *nindikwem;* but first attend to the girl." The old woman began to strip Jade of her wet clothing. Somehow Jade didn't feel embarrassed in front of either of them. Then the woman led her to a room and placed her in a bed, already warmed. The woman had indeed been waiting for her.

"Wait a moment before you try to sleep. You must have some hot broth," she coaxed, as she spooned the hot mixture into Jade's mouth. "It nourishes body and spirit."

Jade had trouble getting it past her swollen throat, but forced as much of it down as she could. She began to lose her grip on reality again, but this time she felt pleasantly drowsy. As she sank into the bed beneath the sheets and blanket, she smelled the pungent, citrus-like aromas of lavender and pine, and wild roses, clean and pleasant to her senses. Jade felt she could stay here forever, in this bed, in this house, in this glade. But one thought gnawed at her mind before she drifted off into a deep, comfortable sleep. This place was the place of her vision, of that she was certain. This cottage, although she had not seen much of it, was the cottage of her vision, but--the woman was not. The black void claimed her.

The old woman returned to the room in which the Indian stood waiting. "It is still beautiful here, is it not?" she asked him now.

"Only because you have made it so," he replied warmly. "That is why I like to visit."

"Bah," she replied lightheartedly. "You know you come to see me, Old Man. Soon I will be joining you and you won't have to visit me here."

He smiled at her tenderly. "But we will come here together when we are needed, yes?"

She nodded. "Just as you come when you know I need you. It is about Jason that I am worried now. *Mawadishiwe*, he visits," she told him. "But I have fear that he is too much of the non-native world. He loses his Indian-ness."

"No," the Indian said softly. "When he needs them, the old ways come through. That is why he is a good police officer. He has the caring and the intuition when he needs them. *Minobimaadizi*," he told her. "He is a good man. You must remember, *nindikwem*, he is part European. He is the way of the new world.

"We cannot stop what has been decreed. What was written in the time before time. We can only help out when he needs us. Soon he will need us no longer, then we will have our peaceful life together. They have both been through much, but they are learning quickly, and they will pass on that wisdom to the next generation."

She nodded, relieved that she could talk to him of Jason. "He will be here soon," she told him. "When he discovers the girl he will be happy. She doesn't know it yet, but she will be happy also. Their true happiness, though, will come a little later. She has not met all her problems yet, nor has he." As he nodded, she looked at him and smiled tenderly. "I love you," she told him gently. "As much now as years ago when we were young together."

"I love you too," he returned. "As much now that you are an old woman as I did when we were young together." He tried to inject a note of humor into their talk, for he knew that she longed to be with him again, to love and to laugh.

"And will I be as young and pretty as you are handsome?" she queried him now, picking up on his tone. She knew what he was doing and understood.

"You may be as young and pretty as you wish," he said. "Do you not remember the Before Time, Old Woman?" He changed the subject without waiting for a reply. "Do you recognize the clothes I am wearing?"

She smiled and nodded. "Those were the first clothes I ever made for you." She smiled at the remembrance. "If I recall, you chose later to wear the jacket with blue jeans. *We must keep up with the times*, you argued." And she mimicked him as he had been forty years before.

"I must go," he told her gently. "But I will be back for you."

She smiled happily, knowing that the next time he came, she would join him. Suddenly there was a knock at her door, and without further words, the Indian vanished.

"*Nookomis*, my grandmother," Jason rasped. "I have need of you."

"Welcome, *noozhishe*, my grandson," she murmured tenderly. "I have been waiting for you." She put her brown, wrinkled arms around him and led him gently into the cottage. "The one for whom you seek is here."

He was stunned. "How did she get here? I thought she was still in the bush."

"Sh, sh," she scolded. "Never question the ways of the Wise Ones." Her eyes sparkled with years of gentle humor. "You should know better than to ask such questions. She is sleeping off a fever now. You might as well have a cup of tea."

"I must see her."

"I know, *noozhishe*, but I expect you out of there in five minutes," she cautioned with a mock sternness in her ancient, wise eyes.

"Grandmother!" He was only half embarrassed. "Five minutes," he agreed laughingly. "And I will need something stronger than tea."

"Tea or nothing," she admonished him. "You do not need alcohol, my grandson. Your spirit is strong enough as it is. What is it the white Europeans call drink? Dutch Courage? No. You have no need of that."

He grinned. He had never been able to get the better of his grandmother, she who had raised him and guided him wisely throughout the years. Why didn't he find the time to visit more often? It wasn't that far from Toronto to Marten River. Five hours and he could be here. Even as he thought it, he knew what it was. Every time he came back he was torn between the two worlds. At least in Toronto he could fit in without having to brood about which world he belonged to. In Toronto he could be just exactly what he was at any given moment without worrying about whether he was Ojibway or Scots, Indian or white. He knew others, of course, who hadn't been able to fit in; but for him it had been easy.

Perhaps, it was that his two natures blended so easily together in Toronto, or that his job permitted the blending of his two backgrounds. Whatever it was, for him it had worked out quite well. His grandmother had been content to stay in the north where she felt she belonged. She would have been despondent in the city. He had asked her early on in his career to join him, but she had declined. "This is my home, Jason. There is no other." But he knew that this life could never be his for very long. He longed for the action of the city, just as much as every so often he longed for the peace of his grandmother's cottage.

He looked down at Jade as she lay curled in deep sleep, induced, he suspected, by his grandmother's special healing broth. Her head and face were swollen, but she was sleeping peacefully now. Gently he sat on the edge of the bed and took her hand. A painful lump welled in his throat. "Jade, my beloved," he whispered. As he slowly became aware that she was naked between the sheets, he became aroused. No wonder his grandmother had admonished him to stay only five minutes!

There was an easy camaraderie between him and his grandmother, born of years of interaction, love, and trust. She had guided him, making sure he learned his native heritage; yet at the same time she recognized that he was of two worlds. For the sake of his Scots ancestors, she had made him learn that heritage too. He felt it only appropriate that he control his wayward hormones before he joined his grandmother in the other room. As he entered, a smile twitched at his lips.

She laughed girlishly at him and tapped him teasingly in his midriff. "Behave yourself," she chided him with the ever-present twinkle in her eye. "The time will come. But not yet. Come, have a cup of tea with an old woman."

"Grandmother, you are not old."

"Don't patronize me, Grandson," she chided as she poured the tea. "Don't tell an old lady she's not old. She knows as well as anyone how old she is. When one is old and no longer fits in with the world, when physical strength wanes, it is time to leave. My time will come soon."

Jason started to protest, but she stopped him with a lifted hand. "I want to go," she said. "Now, drink your tea. Jade will sleep until morning. You can talk to her then. And that is all you will do," she chided. He didn't promise anything, but didn't think that anything would happen between him and Jade in his grandmother's house. He had too much finesse for that, he hoped. Besides, Jade would still be furious with him when she woke up.

He spent a restless night, looking in every hour or two on Jade. In between his visits, he knew his grandmother was looking in on her, too. Near dawn, he fell into an exhausted sleep, just as Jade, her natural good health and buoyancy restored, was awake, feeling refreshed and happy.

Jade knew without any doubt that she was in the cottage of her vision. She felt contented, but she was also curious. As she became more fully awake, she looked through the window to the open area that surrounded the house. Red and pink poppies edged the grassy lawn just before the bush was allowed its rightful place. She bounced to an east-facing window, standing naked and unashamed as she let the morning sun wash over her body. "Good morning, sunshine," she chirruped happily. Just then the door opened and the old woman came in.

"Ah, you are better, I see." She smiled at Jade, who recognized her from the night before.

"Yes, thank you," Jade smiled gratefully. Her face had lost some of its swelling and she could see from both eyes. "But I still don't know how I got here."

"Yes, you do," the Indian woman returned. "But you just haven't accepted the fact yet. You will, when you've lived a little more. You have the inner knowledge. Now," she resumed briskly, "first, here are your clothes. I washed and dried them last night. We can't let Jason see you like that."

"Jason? Here?" A tremor of passion burst through her. She felt the quickening of her body, and rushed to put on her clothes before the woman noticed.

But the woman had, and was pleased. It was a good sign that the two young people felt that way about each other. She hadn't missed Jason's arousal the night before, however much he had tried to hide it. That meant that what they felt was not all in the mind on a rational level, as happened so often these days. What they felt for each other was at an inner level, an animal level with the spirit's acquiescence. It was good, she saw. This was the way all intermingling should be. Spirit and body. Just one or the other always led to disaster.

"Come, you will be hungry," she coaxed Jade. "Jason is still asleep; he kept checking you throughout the night." That she had also been up to tend to Jade didn't seem to trouble her, and she felt no need to mention it to the girl now.

Jade wondered, modestly, if she had been covered at all times. She blushed as she asked his grandmother.

"Would it have made a difference?" the woman asked.

"No." Jade was startled by her own answer. She hesitated. There was something else she had to clear up. "Are you Jason's grandmother?"

Jason's grandmother smiled and nodded. She led Jade into a small eating area off the kitchen where coffee was gurgling through the coffee maker, and bacon and eggs were keeping warm in the electric oven. The cottage, Jade noticed, seemed to have all the modern conveniences.

Sensing her curiosity, Grandmother answered her unasked question. "Jason bought me all these appliances when he started to work. Even though we got along fine without them for years. Don't tell him I said so, but I do appreciate them, especially now I'm older."

The woman pointed to a small room between the bedrooms and what was, Jade could see, a small laundry room. "The bathroom is in there. But I don't think I need to tell you. You've been here before."

Jade pondered the woman's matter-of-fact comment as she used the facility and had a quick shower. Wiping the steam-fogged mirror above the sink, she examined the reduced swelling of her face and noticed the Indian woman had cleaned and re-bandaged her scalp wound. The old woman seemed to know so much about her, and no one, not even Jason, could have told the woman about her vision.

She returned to the kitchen a scant fifteen minutes after she left, eager to hear more of what the intriguing native woman had to say. Jade felt an immediate bonding with the woman, and she was sure the feeling was mutual. Looking at the grandmother closely, Jade could see that the woman had a love for all life. It showed in the lines of her face and the depths of her eyes. "How do you know so much about me?"

The other woman smiled. "When you are as old as I am now, you will have the same powers, my child. But for now, you must experience life; your powers at the moment are limited, and that is good. Too much strength at an early age can do you more harm than good." She placed a loving hand on Jade's arm. "I love my grandson," she said simply. "Be good to him, trust him; he too is wise."

"I . . . we . . ." Jade blundered, unsure of what to say. How could she tell the grandmother that she and Jason had just met, and as yet the only thing that had happened was that she and Jason had kissed--and fought? She wasn't even sure if the loving had really happened or whether it was in her head, conjured up by her deep need.

"I know," the grandmother forestalled her. "But the time will come . . ."

"Tell me," Jade interrupted, more to get around an embarrassing moment than from curiosity. "How do I know so much about this cottage?" She told the old woman of her vision. "The only thing that is different is that the woman I met wasn't you."

Jason's grandmother smiled, but said nothing for a few seconds. Then, "I know what you saw; but if I tell you, it will frighten you."

Jade was about to pop her third piece of crisp bacon into

her mouth. At the other woman's words, her hand went suddenly still in mid-air. "What do you mean?" she managed to force out.

"It's all right," the grandmother soothed. "Everything will be well for you. It is just that you are not ready to hear details yet. You will be, soon, but not yet. Today," she said brightly. "Today is a day of sunshine and love. Come, let's let Jason sleep for a time while we look at the house and the garden."

Jade felt as comfortable with Jason's grandmother as she ever had with anyone and as comfortable with the cottage as she had ever felt anywhere. For some reason that she didn't want to analyze, the words *I'm home, I'm home* kept lilting through her head and heart as she followed Jason's grandmother throughout the house and yard. She noted, however, as they strolled through the gardens, a discrepancy between this cottage and her vision. In her vision the driveway had been of asphalt, while this one was gravel close to the house, trailing off into only packed earth nearer the highway. She wondered whether such a minor variance was worth noting, as everything else held such a magical quality, yet she couldn't ignore it completely.

The two women spent most of the morning chatting and drinking coffee. Jade reveled in the warmth seeping into her and could feel her raw nerves beginning to heal. It was noon before they called a halt to their getting-acquainted chats. "Remember, you must call me Grandmother, just as Jason does," the old woman said, touching Jade's cheek gently. "Now, let's get Jason up and see what the rest of the day brings."

Grandmother took Jason in a cup of coffee, telling Jade that Jason always slept in the nude and she didn't think either one of the young people was up to her seeing him that way yet. "I'm old," she continued. "Things like that don't excite me anymore, but I still remember what it was like to be young." She woke Jason, then returned to the kitchen to chat with Jade.

Jason gulped his coffee while listening to their voices carry through the closed door. Then hastily he dressed. Even though he had wakened several times in the night, he still felt refreshed and ready to put finish to this case. He tried to look nonchalant as he sauntered into the kitchen in search of breakfast, although upon looking at his watch, he decided to combine breakfast and lunch into one huge brunch. His pose wasn't that effective, for as soon as he saw Jade, he became almost as an adolescent again. Grandmother kept up a steady stream of conversation, with Jade interrupting only to tell Jason that his grandmother wouldn't tell her how she had come to be at the cottage.

"I have learned," he told her, only half in jest, "never to question the ways of the Wise Ones." He hoped this bit of news would elicit no startled response from his grandmother, as it had been only the night before that he had questioned her. Her eyes, glinting with amusement, showed him that his remark did not pass her by. Jade looked from one to the other, aware of undertones in the conversation between grandmother and grandson. She noticed that the grandmother's eyes were of the same obsidian black as her grandson's, but there the similarity ended. If anything, Jason looked more Scots than Ojibway, even with his straight dark hair.

She was more than satisfied to hear that Rick had been placed under arrest and was probably in the North Bay jail at that very moment, but was disquieted to learn that Len was still in the bush. To think that he had been in there while she was tramping through it the night before made her shudder. She closed her mind to the pictures. She didn't want to think of Rick and Len yet, and told both the grandmother and Jason that. "I need time," she said, "Time to just absorb what is here today." She looked from Jason to his grandmother, who nodded knowingly.

Jason ate his hearty breakfast-lunch quickly, then excused himself. "I have to let Tom know you're all right," he told Jade now. "I telephoned last night, once I knew you were here, but they're waiting for a detailed report. I should have given it last night," he added guiltily, looking at his watch.

"I'm sure they would know that everything is all right, as you haven't called in," his grandmother volunteered. "You can telephone from here, you know."

Jason gave a noncommittal grunt and, shoving his feet into a pair of casual shoes, quickly left. He needed to get away from the cottage; With Jade in his immediate vicinity, he was finding it increasingly hard to do any logical thinking. He wanted to travel to North Bay to speak to Tom, rather than telephone him, but looking again at his watch, he felt he had better phone him--and quickly. Finding a telephone booth outside a small general store, he put through the call.

He waited as Tom was called to the telephone, and then listened with a sickening feeling as Tom acknowledged, in a somewhat distant manner, Jason's information about finding Jade with his grandmother. Tom responded with the information that Len had been picked up only about an hour before by the K-9 unit. When Tom asked him to come down to the office for a talk, Jason tried to get more information out of his friend, but Tom adamantly refused to prolong the telephone conversation, leaving Jason mystified.

Jason had no recourse but to travel to the OPP detachment, mulling over all the possible motives Tom might have for wanting to see him in person. He had wanted the interval away from Jade, but, perversely, now that he had an enforced one, he wanted nothing more than to be with her at his grandmother's house.

It was after midnight before he returned, weary and upset, to his grandmother's, having turned down Tom's offer of a bed for the night. He needed to think, and in Tom's house he would have to be civil to people. He didn't feel like being civil. He felt like choking someone, but he wasn't sure who was more deserving of his wrath. When they had been questioned after being taken into custody, both Rick and Len, in separate interviews, had implicated Jade in the trafficking of the drugs, and had disavowed any knowledge of the homicide.

Jason thought now of the welts along Jade's face, and when he thought of Len's hands on her, bile rose in his throat. Talk about a dilemma. He believed in Jade, yet he wondered how he could go against all the other professionals in the departments who suspected her. After all, Derek and his crew must have had reasons for their deep suspicion that she knew more than they could prove. He was still trying to solve the problem and sort through what seemed like a whole library of data when he arrived in his grandmother's driveway.

Fortunately, both Jade and his grandmother were asleep. He couldn't possibly face either one yet. Tom had told him to go with his gut feeling. Well, his gut feeling was that Jade was innocent. He knew it would take some time to clear her name, and wondered if she could stand up to all the questioning again. If the issue came to a head, he would want to stand by her. Now all he needed to do was convince her of his loyalty. They needed to talk, to sort through their emotions, but so far, both had been avoiding it.

Quietly he entered the house, slipped off his shoes, and headed for the room that his grandmother always kept in readiness for him. At the moment it seemed the only stable element in his unstable world, and he knew that for the next while he would need all the reinforcement that was offered.

CHAPTER   EIGHT

Jason tossed and turned throughout the night until the early dawn light at last forced him out of bed. He wanted to talk to Jade quietly, maybe get her by herself in the garden she seemed to adore. He had spent most of the night going over in his mind how he would broach the subject. Looking in the mirror, he was surprised to notice grey in his morning stubble and an ashen appearance to his increasingly wrinkled face. The last few days had aged him more than the previous ten years. He hadn't noticed before how time was catching up to him. As he neared the kitchen, he heard his grandmother and Jade happily chatting while preparing breakfast. A guilty feeling swept over him as he overheard Jade recounting to his grandmother all the latest news and gossip of Toronto. Usually his grandmother relied on him for this information. Hearing about happenings on television or radio was not the same to her as hearing it from another. He could relate to that. The media lacked the personal touch of one-on-one opinion of events.

As he approached, he noticed that Jade looked much healthier than she had the previous day. Her face was clearing nicely and she looked more rested, although all the strain of the past few days had not yet left her features. His grandmother's cottage, he knew, was working its magic on her just as it did on everyone who visited. If his mirror image was anything to go by, it hadn't quite worked for him yet.

He accepted a cup of coffee from his grandmother, who greeted him with, "You were late getting in last night." He hadn't heard that from her since he had been a teenager. Now he was too upset to even grin, and he turned away from her discerning look.

"Would you two young people pick me some strawberries after you have your breakfast?" she asked them. "There's a wild patch on the other side of the stream and a few of them are already ripe. Jason knows where it is."

He did. The berries were on the opposite side of the glade, in an open area, yet shielded from the house by a copse of white birch and poplar. He looked at his grandmother. "I have to talk with Jade."

She eyed him speculatively. "You can do it while you're picking the berries. It's beautiful outdoors. But this morning I think I will stay in and take a little catnap. These old bones are getting more tired every day."

Jason ignored his grandmother's allusion to her health, knowing that it was just a ploy. True, she did seem more frail each time he saw her, but there was still a vibrant flame burning within her. He marveled at her perspicacity but frowned as Jade offered to do the dishes. He knew she didn't want to be alone with him. Well, he couldn't blame her, but he had to talk to her about Tom's revealing information.

His grandmother shooed them out of her way. "Dishes can wait," she said. "Young people cannot." Jade did the dishes anyway, much to his grandmother's disgust and Jason's growing frustration.

He swallowed, knowing his grandmother was trying to get him and Jade together. It wasn't going to happen. "It's not the right moment, yet," he said to his grandmother, apropos of nothing Jade could discern. He noticed Jade intercept the look between woman and grandson at his comment.

"It is never the right or the wrong time," she advised him. "It just happens. In my day," she continued, "we wouldn't have stopped to do such mundane things as dishes. We would have taken the time to enjoy the flowers and the sunshine. And each other." She added the last item with emphasis.

Jade smiled tentatively, unable to follow a conversation in which much of what passed between grandmother and grandson remained unspoken, soul level to soul level. Instead she concentrated on her surroundings. She felt comfortable in the lovely kitchen with the pale gold-colored walls that captured the sunlight. The whole ambience of the house was one of brightness and light and inner warmth.

Throughout, there was a scattering of furnishings of palest green with touches of a soft shade hovering between brick and rose. The floors were all in a wood that Jade couldn't identify, finished in what she recognized as Varathane. If modern is better, go for it, Jade thought to herself. Even with all the light colors and bare wooden floors on which there were rugs of various sizes, all in pale shades of green and the rose color, the house was warm.

It helped, Jade thought, to have the many windows facing in all directions, so that they framed the sun-soaked glen from every angle. The view would be as colorful in the autumn as now, or stunning in the winter when wet snow draped the branches in froths of white.

She acknowledged to herself, as she let her thoughts wander in irrelevancies, that she was evading the real issue--time alone with Jason. She was afraid to leave this house. In here was refuge, out there was danger. Deep down she knew that the next few hours would change her life irrevocably, and she didn't know whether she could hang on to her sense of self for much longer. She had a feeling that she would lose her innermost being once she stepped outside the cottage. Steeling herself against the inevitable, she chided herself for being a coward. She knew she couldn't stay in the house forever, and she hoped that, somehow, she would dredge up the courage when she needed it most.

Jason interrupted her self-absorption. "Come on," he cajoled, "Grandmother wants some strawberries for a pie." He grabbed a plastic pail and a worn and faded red blanket from the laundry room. He, too, was reluctant to begin the conversation, for he knew that from Jade's point of view, it wouldn't be a conversation, but the same type of accusatory grilling to which she had already been subjected in Toronto. He didn't have the heart or the guts to tell her that she would have to go in for questioning, and figured if he postponed it for an hour or so, no great catastrophe would ensue.

"Do we really need a blanket to pick strawberries? You're getting soft from city living," Jade teased him, hoping to erase the mantle of apprehension that was descending over her.

Jason had his motives clear in his own mind. He had to find a way to get her to open up about Toronto and Derek without arousing her suspicions. "I often sit by the stream when I come here, just listening to my thoughts in the water," he confided to her, hoping Jade would see he was on the same wave length as she.

She looked at him, amazed. Never would she have suspected the macho cop to have the sentiments he had just expressed, although with a small tremor of shock she realized he had already shown a tender side she hadn't expected. Giving his grandmother an anxious look, she followed Jason out the door.

After the rain of two days before, everything smelled fresh. The Iceland poppies and tall valerian, having been battered and cowed by the heavy rains, were springing upright again. Jason led her across the grass to the stream. "I'm not going to carry you," he teased. "You're going to have to jump from stepping stone to stepping stone. You would probably prefer that, anyway, as you seem to be one of the members of the liberated set."

She did as she was told, hiking up her jeans and removing her shoes, but did not let him get away with treating her in such a cavalier fashion. "Last night I was carried across in the arms of a handsome young Native," she informed him haughtily.

"Who?" He startled her by grabbing her arm.

"I don't know." She looked at him in surprise. "Your grandmother seemed to know him quite well. I don't remember that much about him, except that he led me through the bush to this cottage. I was soaked, feverish, and delirious. Maybe I just dreamed that's what happened," she qualified. "But I didn't get wet in the stream," she added roguishly, with not a little doubt about her own memory.

For some reason he couldn't comprehend, Jason was unnerved by what she had said, but he forced himself to shrug it off and dismissed the whole thing from his mind. If his grandmother knew the man, he must be all right. He turned his smiling face to her now. "Look, here are the strawberries Grandmother likes to use for her pie." He pointed to a large patch where the wild strawberries were three times as large as any wild ones she had ever seen. "For some reason, they grow well here," he added unnecessarily.

He put the pail on the ground beside him and started to pick, postponing as long as possible the time when he would have to talk about what was entrenched in his mind. Jade joined him, relishing the serenity. The sun soaked into her back, not yet hot enough to cause discomfort, but warm enough to caress her worn nerves.

The stream percolated happily over the rocks and disappeared through the bush on its way to a rendezvous farther south. Overhead, hidden in the trees, a warbler started to sing, but suddenly stopped; a hawk circled above, its predatory appetite whetted. Jade noticed several smaller birds take the offensive against its marauding maneuvers. A large monarch butterfly fluttered past her, just as a ruby-throated hummingbird dipped its bill into some wild purple bergamot thriving beside the nurturing and nourishing stream.

Jade felt herself in a time warp. This place and this time were years removed from her work and life in Toronto. In fact, it was removed from the events of two days ago. Drowsy from the sun and the fresh air, she noticed they had half filled the large pail with the berries.

"Well, I did, anyway," Jason grinned when she commented on the large number of berries they had picked. "You, lazy bones, are a terrible berry-picker."

She drew back to give him a mock punch on his arm, and as she let go to land a soft whap on his biceps, he grabbed her arm and gently pulled her to him. She looked at him, half drowsily, half wonderingly, her lips parted in anticipation. As he bent his head to touch her lips with his, a white-hot bolt of lightning shot through her.

She had felt this way only once before, and that was the brief time with Jason in Aunt Kate's cottage, a scene she now banished from her mind. Indeed, she could think of very little anyway. Her whole body was suffused with feeling, her senses attuned to the man who was planting tender kisses behind her ear.

He ran his lips down her flesh to the crew neck of her T-shirt. "Jade," he murmured thickly, "Oh, Jade, honey, you're beautiful." His hand slipped under her shirt and caressed her back, sending warm quivers throughout her whole being. She writhed under his touch, craving more but not knowing exactly what she wanted. These feelings were all so new to her. Even Derek hadn't aroused her this way. In fact, now that she had a comparison, Derek had not aroused her at all. The knowledge flashed through her like an earthquake. Maybe that was why he had told her to get lost, she speculated briefly. No one had ever aroused her as this man was doing.

Jason had removed her shirt, and pressed her gently down onto the blanket. A small mountain ash tree gave dappled shade that kept them out of the reaches of the ever-warming sun. Jade wasn't certain whether it was the sun that was warming quickly or whether it was she who was heating up. She felt Jason's wiry chest hairs against her tender breasts, arousing her so that her nipples were distended as hard nubs. She was teetering on the edge of ecstasy.

But that was before Jason undid the snap on her jeans and eased them over her newly-sensitive hips. He stroked her, his hand gliding back and forth over her flat stomach and then down to her soft pulsating flesh. He continued to caress her until she was a mass of sensations and she moved her stomach against his hand in an eons-old undulating motion, wanting to quell the deep primeval ache inside her. She pushed against him, feeling herself moist between her thighs.

Sometime, she didn't know when, he had divested himself of his own jeans and shoes. He lay over her as she arched her back to meet him. Her hands stroked his shoulders, and she was at once frightened and eager. His aroused manhood pulsed against his white briefs. She urgently maneuvered the last vestiges of his clothing down over his hips, surprising herself by her tentative forwardness. He was poised to enter her body, and she could wait no longer, but rose to meet him just as he entered into her. Jade felt a moment of pain which quickly disappeared among all her heightened senses. He had paused momentarily, seemingly stunned, and in that time, she let herself relax and revel in the sensation of his throbbing within her.

"Jade," he murmured. "Oh, Jade, honey. . . . Why?"

Whatever he was going to say was cut off in their mutual desire for release. Together, their souls rose to the sunlit sky until Jade could no longer tell whether it was day or bright night. The woods, the glen, the birds coalesced into one, and she and Jason were part of the shimmering white and blue sky.

She wanted to sob and laugh at the same time. Instead, she moaned his name repeatedly until the final release when everything was still. As their wildly beating hearts slowed, Jason's mind was in turmoil as he looked at Jade lying content from their lovemaking. They lay for several moments in each other's arms until the sun reached its highest point.

Jason forced all his professional thoughts to arm's length, not allowing them to intrude into his time with Jade, but he was acutely aware that they lurked on the outskirts of his mind, waiting their turn.

After several minutes he picked her up tenderly and waded into a deeper part of the stream where he set her on her feet. She felt the flat cool stones on the bottom of the stream, and stood contentedly in the waist-high water while it rippled over both their bodies and removed the traces of their love-making. The cooling waters glided over her body like a silk scarf or a lover's caress.

Jason looked at her fondly, but also somewhat ruefully. "You were a virgin," he remarked blandly. "That's something I never expected." Before Jade could ask him defensively what he meant by that remark, he forestalled her by kissing her lightly. "I just didn't think there were any women your age who waited these days."

"Well, I did," Jade replied coolly, losing some of the rapture of their lovemaking. "Derek and I were never lovers--more his reluctance than mine, probably."

As he continued to caress her with the cool water, he picked a handful of wild mint and rubbed it over her body, imparting a bracing sensation that did nothing to cool her ardor; if anything it aroused her more. He let the mint leaves fall into the water where they swirled away in the gentle current. Grasping another handful, he handed them to her to rub him as he had done to her. She started to rub them into his back, afraid to touch his front, but he turned abruptly and guided her hand with his. It took every ounce of will power he had not to make love to her again. He crushed her to him, breathing deeply and knew she was as aroused as he.

"Mm, that's gorgeous." Jade abandoned herself to the sensuous feel of the cooling mint as its pungent aroma seeped into every newly awakened pore. Her problems of the past few days and years slipped away, and she resisted the temptation to be hurt by Jason's remark, letting her mind go blank and her senses come to life.

Jason led her back to the blanket, where she curled against him, secure in his warmth. She felt his intense arousal again and wriggled against him, inviting more intimate touches, but he refused to give in to her timid invitation, and both dozed in the warm dappled shade. By the time they awoke, they were hot from the sun. He wanted to make love to her again, but knew that it was not the time.

A feeling of dread washed over him, refusing to be sloughed off. It had never been like this before, and he knew that there was a chemistry between them that they had both felt from the beginning, and that Tom and Grandmother both recognized. He helped Jade up and picked up the blanket and the pail of berries. Jade, still in a tranquil state, followed him back to the cottage, pondering why she had felt apprehensive about leaving the house. The outcome certainly hadn't been what she had anticipated, but far more earth shattering by far. If only it had not been marred by Jason's surprised comment.

When they returned to the cottage with the pail still only half full of berries, his grandmother was waiting for them with a frown on her usually serene face. Expecting a remark about the pail being only half filled, Jason had been trying to devise a tale about how sparse the crop was this year. But one look at his grandmother's face and he knew there was trouble.

"Your friend Tom just called in for you, very upset. He wants you to meet him as soon as possible. Jason, what's wrong?"

Jason turned pale. Suddenly, his euphoria was completely gone. He turned to Jade. "I want you to stay here with Grandmother while I go to Tom's," he commanded her.

Jade looked at him, mutinous over his tone and still with a lingering resentment over his remark. "I can't stay here, however much I would like to." She smiled weakly at Jason's grandmother. "I want to get my car and return to Toronto."

Jason's face registered his unease. "Toronto? Why Toronto?"

"Because my job is there," Jade told him with an air of impatience. "Bernie was kind enough to give me time off, but he's not going to like it if I stay away indefinitely."

Jason looked at her in a new light. "I had forgotten that you had a job."

Jade checked herself from asking how he thought she managed to rent an apartment in Toronto and own her red sports car. She felt she knew what his answer would be, and that was another reason she had to return to Toronto. He still did not trust her; that was apparent in his remark about her virginity. She looked at him and saw that he was struggling to get something said.

"Jade, they want to question you at North Bay. I've been trying to find a way to tell you."

Her face whitened even more. "What are you saying?" she whispered.

"I'm saying that Rick and Len both implicated you in the

drug trafficking." Ignoring her gasp, he pushed on. "That's what Tom wanted me for yesterday. I was supposed to have you back down there early this morning."

"Oh, Jason!" His grandmother's outburst went unheeded by both of them.

"When did you intend to tell me?" Jade asked in a deceptively quiet voice, oblivious to his grandmother's disappointed face. "You're no better than the two men in jail."

He knew what she was talking about and felt like the scum to which she likened him. "Believe me, I never intended for anything to happen. And I don't recall your fighting me off, either." He was nearly yelling, trying to foist some of his guilt onto her. It wasn't working. He cleared his throat nervously, then continued at a more refined level. "I'll have to drive you down, at least as far as Tom's. Your car's at his place. They found it hidden in the bush about three kilometers from your aunt's cottage. Other than a few scratches, it's okay."

He couldn't stand the sick, shocked look on her face, which he knew was not caused by the news about her car. If he had thought that his grandmother's place was doing her good, he castigated himself, he had certainly undone any benefits that had taken place. There was nothing more to say, except good-bye to his grandmother.

In a daze, Jade took her leave of the elderly woman. She knew that the grandmother understood, especially when the lovely old lady gently squeezed her hand. "All will work out, my child." She smiled enigmatically at Jade and kissed them both good-bye.

Jade could not constrain herself any longer. "I don't know how you can bear to kiss this pig of a grandson of yours." She turned and stormed out the door. Jason felt his embarrassment color his face, but his grandmother didn't seem to be insulted at all. She probably agreed with

Jade.

The ride to Tom's house was accomplished quickly and, for the most part, in silence. Jade observed that most of their rides together took place in an atmosphere of animosity. This silent ride wasn't helped any when Jason said: "I just found out Derek's undercover with Narcotics Division." She was left speechless.

Reaching Tom's house, both were relieved to discover that the adults weren't home. They met only one of Tom and Lorraine's young sons, who greeted them like a friendly puppy. He was disappointed they couldn't stay, and it was clear to Jade that he looked up to Jason in hero worship. Well, somebody had to like him, she supposed. They stopped only long enough to advise Tom's son to let his parents know they had picked up Jade's car. She said good-bye to Jason coolly, hesitating as though she wanted to say more, then with a wistful sigh turned away and sped off in her car.

She had wanted to tell Jason that she was attracted to him; in fact, she felt that the emotion went deeper than that. Until now, she had never let another man come even close to making love to her. She might have let Derek, she knew that. Or maybe she wouldn't have when the time had come. She couldn't envision making love to any other man but Jason, and because of this, she felt that she had to get as far away from him as possible--for both their sakes. Whether she liked it or not, Jason was a police officer, and she knew that once it was found out that the two of them had a serious relationship going, that would be the end of Jason's career. She would have to get her name cleared first, and she wasn't sure she knew how to do that except to keep telling the truth.

Whether or not Jason had kept her under surveillance didn't matter anymore. It didn't even hurt, for when she had looked at him, she had realized that he was just as miserable as she was over the whole incident at the cottage.

She hoped that she could get to North Bay and give her story and then get back to Toronto. It was highly ironic, she mused, that she was bolting back to Toronto, when in the normal course of events, she usually bolted away from it. She took a last look out her window at Jason and drove ahead of him to the North Bay detachment.

He, too, was at a loss for the words that would make their world all right again. There was so much that he wanted to tell her--how much he loved her, that he believed in her, that he wanted her, but he knew she was in no mood to hear it, and he was in no position to say it. He was still an officer, sworn to uphold the law, and he was still involved in the case, whether he wanted to be or not.

For Jade, the drive back to Toronto was uneventful. She spent the hours contemplating the events of the last few days. Where Jason was, she didn't know. He might still have been in the Marten River area or North Bay, though his presence there was not required at the moment. Their parting had been rather cool. Jade inhaled deeply and let her breath out on one long sigh.

Poor Tom hadn't known what to say, either, except that he trusted Jason to make the right choice. Jade wasn't sure what to make of that remark. Whether Tom had been on her side or not, she didn't know. At first, she rather felt that he had, but in his capacity, he had to remain neutral.

She had been waiting her turn when Jason came through the door after his briefing with Tom at the North Bay office. He had hesitated, but she had turned her head away. Neither of them had known what to say.

The three-and-a-half hour drive was conducive to deep inner thoughts. When she and Jason had made love, their lovemaking had been warm and tender and passionate. They had both wanted it. What Jason had said afterwards in the heat of anger and guilt had been true. She had wanted him every bit as much as he wanted her, maybe more. She couldn't blame him entirely. But to come from that euphoria to this despair was too abrupt for Jade to handle.

True, she had been more than willing to dampen their relationship, especially after she found she was still implicated in the cocaine dealing. But to know that Jason had wanted the cooling period, too, was something that Jade had not counted on.

Turning off at Stellar Avenue, she negotiated the turn until she came to the house in North York. She had been fortunate when she had first come to the city. Through an acquaintance in North Bay, Jade had heard of a young widow who owned a new home and wanted someone to share it to help pay her mortgage. The partnership had worked out well for both of them. The woman had designated the finished basement as Jade's apartment and maintained everything else. Her landlady did not interfere in Jade's life and Jade never intruded into her landlady's, and Jade had a standard of living that she couldn't have afforded elsewhere in the vicinity of the outrageously expensive provincial capital.

She now swung her car into the drive, glad that Irene wasn't home, because she couldn't face anyone. She wanted nothing more than to sit alone to contemplate this last disaster in her life. During the long drive, when she had gone over the events of the last few days, she hadn't allowed her mind to dwell on Jason's grandmother's home. This vision-becoming-reality was private, and had to have all her concentration. Jade was sure that she had never been there before, and wondered if there really was anything to her flashes of intuition.

The cottage was still a puzzle. Much about the whole period while she was there bothered her, but she could not grasp what it was. Now that she was back in her familiar city environment, the whole episode seemed like a dream. It was like going on a vacation and thinking you'll remember all the little highlights, only finding when you return home that you remember very little. She wouldn't even have photographs to jog her memory. The stitches in her head would have to suffice as a reminder.

Over the weekend she reflected upon her past few days in the north and her involvement with Derek in Toronto as she tidied her apartment and prepared to rejoin Bernie in his book store. She wondered if she could turn the harrowing events of her vacation into a short story. But even that, she thought, was beyond her. She was still too raw from the past week and too bruised, physically and emotionally.

She forced herself to call Aunt Kate to tell her some of what had happened over the past few days, omitting any reference to her episode with Rick and Len, and she was still reeling from that phone call. Aunt Kate, while not admitting anything, had not sounded too surprised. Jade didn't understand this. She was sure that her aunt wasn't mixed up in the sordid mess; yet the hurt and shock that Jade had expected had not been in Kate's voice. Her aunt, sensing Jade's uneasiness, promised to fly from Florida on Monday, saying that there was nothing she could do for Rick at that point, anyway, if he had sniffed a little cocaine or smoked a joint of marijuana. Really, it did seem a big fuss to make.

Monday morning, Jade awakened early. She wanted to get back to work, to get back to some normalcy in her day-to-day life. She expected to be summoned for questioning, but felt that if they wanted her badly enough, they could damn well track her down at the book store. At least one son-of-a-bitch at the Toronto Police Department knew where to find her. She was still smarting from learning that Derek had been undercover, hoping she would reveal some tidbit of information about Rick.

There had been no word from Jason in the three days since she had been back. Most of the weekend she had vacillated between expecting him to call and hoping he wouldn't. She looked around her apartment with a new perspective.

The cement block walls had been covered in paneling. Huge windows gathered in the sun, adding coziness to her small refuge. Before her trip to Marten River, she had been content here. She hadn't had her dream in which she had seen the cottage and the elderly woman, and she hadn't visited Jason's grandmother. Now her apartment felt cramped and dark. She felt restless and still baffled over the vision and its meaning.

The cottage in the dream had been the one belonging to Jason's grandmother, but the grandmother had not been the old woman of her vision, and Jade was still trying to analyze the differences between the two.

The more she thought about it, the more she was sure her vision had allowed her a glimpse into a cottage of the past; yet that didn't quite fit, either, for the driveway had been paved and the furnishings of the cottage had been modern.   Also, she couldn't decipher the connection between the cottage and herself. Unless, she muttered darkly as she dressed for work, it had been her psyche telling her that she would lose her virginity there.

Virginity, such an old-fashioned, Victorian word, yet for her it still meant that she had maintained control of herself. She had not been one of the new breed of women who believed it was all right to have sex with several partners. She never questioned her decision, although she knew her friends thought it odd, considering her lifestyle in her formative years.

Her analyst had asked about her lack of a sex life, also, and she was still not able to answer it. Perhaps, she speculated, she felt it was the only thing she had to offer to a man, yet her analyst had assured her that she had more to offer than most people he knew, in therapy or out.

When she arrived at the store, Bernie greeted her with a

hug and a judicious look. "You're different," he commented, looking her in the eye. Then, seeing traces of bruises under her carefully applied makeup, he whistled softly. "I was going to say that you look as though you've fallen in love, but there's more to it than that, isn't there, Kiddo?"

Jade felt duty-bound to tell him about her cousin and the drugs and the murder. Good thing business was slow in the book shop on Monday mornings, Jade thought. Bernie looked at her, aghast. "Wow! Some few days of rest. Why didn't you take another week off? You definitely need a break now," he advised.

She shook her head. The idleness would just allow her more time to think, and that she did not need. "Besides," she told Bernie, "they may want me for questioning or as a witness or something, and I'll need the time off then. I also need an hour or two to have these stitches out." She parted her hair and showed him the fresh bandage.

Bernie gave her a lopsided, sympathetic grin and nodded. "There's a lot more to this holiday story than you're telling me." He held up his hand to forestall any defensive remarks; this was not the time for questions. Jade would have just given him one of her baleful looks and clammed up, drawing into herself as was her habit. Life had not done her any favors so far.

CHAPTER NINE

Jason stayed in North Bay an extra day. As the murder had taken place in the District of Nipissing, the two men were being held in the North Bay jail pending trial. He knew Toronto would have liked to prosecute them for drug trafficking, but as far as he was concerned they would have to wait their turn. Because they had no real evidence that the two men had committed the murder of the girl, the best they could do at the time was arrest Len for shooting at Jason and apprehend Rick for his assault on Jade. They could not arrest either man for stalking Jade. Jason knew better than anyone that with a good lawyer, it would come down to a *he said, she said* situation and both men would get off. The police had gone with their strongest suit.

Once they had the men in custody, Jason had spoken at length with Jade's cousin ascertaining just what role, if any, Jade had played in the drug dealing. He had been ninety-nine percent certain that Jade had been innocent of anything that the two men had been involved in, but he had to make sure. God knew, he loved her, but he knew that if she had been involved he would lose her, and he wanted to resign from the force before that happened. If she had been involved . . . . He didn't want to think about the possibility.

The emotional upheaval of losing another love because of his job would be his undoing. He and his wife had started out in love too, but it hadn't held up through the demands of his work. It had taken him ten years to get past his guilt over her unhappiness and death. Okay, as Tom had said, maybe it did take him longer than anyone else to muster some control over his problem, but he had mastered it long before he met Jade, of that he was sure. He wanted her; he needed her; he was willing to give up his job rather than lose her.

He had questioned Rick with a vengeance, taking three witnesses into the interrogation room with him. He didn't want anyone accusing him of badgering the suspect. Rick had sat staring at him, his usual smirk of superiority spread across his face.

"What difference does it make, cop? You want to get it on with her, too? Half the world wants to lay my beautiful cousin, but she can be mighty choosy."

Jason's stomach had churned at Rick's devaluing outburst. What had taken his and Jade's lovemaking out of the purely *good sex* category was that they truly loved each other. It was their love, both spiritual and sexual, that had made the whole act beautiful. And nothing could destroy that, not even Rick's vulgar mouth.

Jason saw in a sudden flash of insight just what it was that had made Rick hate his cousin so much. The aunt's cottage had been only a part of the reason. Somewhere hidden in the past, she had rejected Rick's advances. He wondered if Jade even recalled the episode. He knew that he would never ask her to remember it--if he ever got to talk to her again.

After Jason had put some heavy psychological pressure on him, Rick admitted that Jade had known nothing about their criminal activities, or as Rick called them, *our little enterprise*. Jason could see that Rick did not think he was doing anything especially evil.

With his court-appointed lawyer beside him, fielding questions and forestalling any incriminating answers, Rick was confident, but Jason pressed on, knowing that Tom was doing the same with Len. Periodically, the two officers took a break from their interrogations and checked each other's progress.

After six grueling hours, when it appeared that neither man would confess to the homicide, Jason had a moment of inventiveness. After Rick's revealing comment about Jade, Jason pretended an empathy with the man that he really didn't have. And this resulted in Rick's revising his earlier statement, much to his lawyer's undisguised dismay.

Jason left the interrogation room and joined Tom in another, passing the tape to his friend with a self-satisfied smile. Tom was able to question Len, having Rick's admission on the cassette he held in his hand. It was just a matter of time before Len admitted his part in the homicide. Jason knew that Len wasn't the strong individual that he believed he was. It was his very weakness that had made him such a willing pawn in Rick's game. Much to the two lawyers' chagrin, they could do nothing to stop the admission of guilt by their clients. Jason tried with an admirable amount of self control not to grin in triumph.

He left North Bay with a lighter step, but was still unable to get up the nerve to call Jade. He preferred to grill felons, face a firing squad, stand up to his captain's explosive wrath, anything other than contact the blond woman he had fallen in love with. He knew he had moved too quickly with her. Hell, they had both moved quickly. They hadn't been able to establish a rapport that hadn't included sex.

Could they ever begin over, he wondered, or was it too late? There was no going back now. It might be better all round to forget her. She had probably made up her mind to forge onward with her own life, relegating him to some corner of her mind where her unpleasant memories were stored. But he knew as soon as he thought it, that he could never forget the long-legged young woman with spun moonlight hair who really wasn't his type at all.

He looked at their relationship from what he thought would be her point of view. All these years she had survived pretty well on her own; she didn't need him. She had a burgeoning career as a writer. And her life skills were superior to anything he had ever before come across. Her stamina and courage were greater than what many people acquire in a life time. With great force of will he forced her out of his mind. The void aggrieved his soul.

Returning to Toronto the day after Jade, he went first to Narcotics Division. He knew the whole station was abuzz with the news of the arrest of the two men. "Would it hurt you guys to let the rest of us know what's going on?" he thundered at the sergeant behind the desk. "It might make it easier in future for me to do your job for you," he added with a derisive sneer.

It was galling to Derek's division to know that Jason had gone to North Bay and Marten River to gather information about the situation surrounding the homicide and had ended up, along with Tom and two officers from North Bay, apprehending the two men wanted in Toronto in connection with drug trafficking.

The Toronto division had maneuvered around the two men for months, thinking they could lure more significant members into their web. That Rick and Len might be responsible for the murder up north had not entered their thinking. They hadn't believed the two men capable of anything but small-time dealing. Perhaps the fact that Rick was related to Jade had kept the suspicion from their minds.

Many of the men and women of the force had met Jade when she was hanging around with Derek. Most had come to like her. Some even had sought her out in the book shop, confirming that their first impressions of her innocence and sincerity had been the correct ones. It may have been that, and Derek's second-hand knowledge of Jade's aunt, that had kept all doubts to a minimum.

In any event, the two men would be questioned further as to their involvement in the drug trade, but the murder would be the main charge, the division head had informed Jason, especially when the homicide division now had an admission of guilt.   It gave them something more substantial to base their case on. Jason was still glowering. He had been sore since he had left Jade in North Bay. He wanted her, but knew he couldn't have her yet, if at all. He frowned at the sergeant now.

"Where's this Derek guy, anyway?" There was nothing he wanted more at the moment, than to plough into the guy and beat him to a pulp, simply because he had been involved with Jade, and Jason wasn't sure whether she still cared for the guy or not. Derek hadn't started his shift yet, and Jason figured that it was Derek's lucky day--at least it delayed the pummeling that Jason had in mind for him for another time.

The desk sergeant gave him a surly glare. "Look, if you're finished giving us hell, how about going back to your own division, and if you want to talk to Derek you can talk to him when he comes into work. I'm not giving you his home address--not in the state you're in." They both knew that Jason could get the address any time he wanted it, but Jason felt the warning in the other's words.

"You're right." He backed down, mumbling an apology. "I just need some sleep." That much was true. He hadn't slept for more than a few hours since the much-needed rest in his grandmother's cottage. "But you can tell Derek that I want to talk to him. Tonight."

Jason strode out of the station and into the hot noon-hour sun. Officially, he was still on holiday. Some holiday, he thought. He would have to go back to work just to rest up. He wanted to go to the book store to see Jade, but was prevented from going by his uncertainty about their relationship. He wanted to tell Jade that she was clear, but knew if he did, she would presume he had believed her guilty. What did he care? He wasn't ready for commitment, anyway. The last ten years without anyone special in his life had been just fine, and he didn't need anybody now. He couldn't quite ignore the hollow feeling deep within when he pulled up to his house.

Jason poured himself a Scotch and paced about his home office until he was sure Derek would be at work. When he could wait no longer, he drove over to the Narcotics Division. Before the blond man had a chance to say anything, Jason verbally attacked him. "What do you mean putting Jade through all that interrogation?" Jason thundered at the man who was trying with difficulty not to grin. Derek had been informed of Jason's impending visit, so was prepared for the outburst. "And why didn't you tell her you're undercover? She thought you were a drug dealer. *I* thought you were a drug dealer, until your office chose to toss me a few bits of information." Jason heard himself becoming louder.

Derek looked at him calmly and shrewdly. "Cool it, Buddy. If you were in my place, would you have done it differently?"

Jason was about to reply in the affirmative, but because he was honest and shrewd himself, he recognized that he would have carried out the investigation in approximately the same way. "No, I guess not," he muttered, forcing himself to calm down.

"Tell me," Derek queried now, pursing his lips. "Why is this girl so important to you? You couldn't have met her more than a week ago at the very most."

"Yeah," Jason affirmed the newness of his relationship with Jade. He wasn't about to add any other details; he was still too confused himself. He couldn't say that he had a relationship with Jade now, because they had effectively ended that. Yet, he wanted to protect her still. Hell, he wanted her still, but he wasn't about to tell Derek any of that. He didn't want what he felt for Jade to be the main topic of discussion in the locker room bantering that took place over casual relationships.

Derek sensed Jason's hesitation and searched the man's dark eyes shrewdly. "Jade and I didn't have a real relationship, you know. She was adrift and looking for something that was missing from her life. I wasn't it. In case you're wondering, we didn't have any physical relationship."

"Yeah, I know." The words slipped out before Jason had thought about what he would say. Derek raised his eyebrows and Jason, seeing the glint of humor in the other's eyes, felt stripped naked and vulnerable.

"Where is she now?" Derek enquired.
Jason raked a hand through his thick black hair. "Here in Toronto; that's all I know. I haven't seen her since she came back from Marten River."

Derek frowned. This was not the Jade he knew. From the rumors he'd heard, the two had been close. The girl he knew would have welcomed a relationship with somebody she could trust. And he knew as he looked at the man before him, that Jade could trust Jason with her life. Derek felt guilty that he had betrayed her trust, yet knew there was nothing he could do to set matters right over that chapter of their lives. Having known Jade, he had a feeling he would be seeing her before very long. Although it had been she who had maneuvered herself into a sort of relationship with him, she wouldn't take his deceit quietly. She would come in and lambaste him just as the detective standing before him had. Good thing he had broad shoulders, he mused with a wry grin. "Is she still at the book shop?" he enquired of Jason now, in what he hoped sounded like a bland question.

Jason nodded, again apologizing. "Look, I'm sorry I came on so strong. This seems to have been getting to me more than it should."

Derek nodded either his agreement or in acceptance of

the apology--Jason wasn't sure which, and didn't much care. They discussed the case for a few minutes longer, carefully avoiding any mention of Jade, with Derek filling him in on the details--why they had kept Jade close at hand, how they had suspected her cousin from the start. Derek's initial visit to the book store had been with the awareness of Jade's connection to Rick. When Jade had pursued a relationship, Derek, with his investigative skills well honed, had sensed that she needed to be close to someone and had taken advantage of that need.

"Do you think the aunt is a mule?" Jason asked now, referring to Jade's Aunt Kate and her frequent trips to Florida.

"We haven't been able to ascertain any connection; I doubt it, but I don't think she's as innocent about this situation as Jade thinks she is."

Jason nodded. "Jade loves her aunt. I hate to think what will happen if she finds out that her aunt is involved in any of this."

Derek went into some of the details he knew of Jade's formative years, and Jason felt a ball of jealousy forming in his gut. He didn't want Derek to know all about Jade's life. There hadn't been time for Jade to tell him much about herself.

"We really didn't have time to talk about things like that," he observed to Derek now. To himself he added, *but we took time to make love, one heavenly interlude of lovemaking that will remain in my soul for a lifetime.* It suddenly came to him that Jade had been right. They didn't know anything about each other. He wanted to take her out to dinner, laugh with her over silly things, gaze with her at an evening sunset. Maybe he could approach her after a suitable time and ask her out on a date. Could they have an ordinary date, or had they passed the point of no return?

Shaking hands with Derek, he sized the other man up

and liked what he saw. He noticed Derek going through the same scrutinizing process. Hell, they were very much alike, Jason saw now, except for their outward appearances. Maybe that's why Jade had seemed to have an affinity with him. Was she still missing Derek, then? Maybe Jason had been a surrogate lover, because Derek had been the one to whom she had first gravitated. Of course, she hadn't known Jason then, but . . . . Jason spoke none of his thoughts aloud. He wasn't about to let Derek in on his insecurities concerning Jade.

As Jason left the station, Derek was frowning with a new thought. He wondered if Jason had told Jade any of the latest details of this case, and he debated whether he should look Jade up and tell her that he thought she should pursue the relationship with the sergeant from the homicide squad.

Giving the matter much thought, he decided against the idea. If there was anything he had learned in his thirty-five years, it was to stay out of other people's lives as much as possible. Live and let live; life was easier that way. Dismissing the whole idea from his mind, he immersed himself again in his work.

The end of August arrived. It had been seven weeks since Jason had seen Jade. He was near desperation, but had been kept occupied with three new homicides, one of which involved the dismembered body parts of a young woman. He wondered how long he could keep going and keep himself emotionally detached from his work. He needed someone to talk to more than ever, someone who would understand his frustration and rage. He needed Jade.

Knowing he would have to return to North Bay to testify at the trial of the two men, it was all he could do to keep the bile from rising each time he thought of Jade's cousin wanting to kill her. He had intuited that Jade had edited many details out of her version of her captivity with Len and Rick when she had related it to him at his grandmother's cottage. Turning into a masochist, he periodically tortured himself with the picture of Len trying to rape her.

To have such hatred for someone as Rick had for Jade was beyond his understanding. He couldn't conceive of Jade evoking that much hatred in anyone, but then he always believed that people couldn't make others react in any particular way--a remnant of his grandmother's philosophy? Or did it go back even farther than that? What was it Eleanor Roosevelt had said? *No one can make you feel inferior without your consent."* It worked for other types of emotions as well. A good philosophy, he had thought then, and thought so now.

It effectively placed all blame for one's actions squarely on the individual who perpetrated them. So he didn't sympathize with Rick at all. As far as Jason was concerned, Jade's cousin wanted to feel hurt and abused; he wouldn't choose any other way to be. It was great to feel that everyone else was to blame for your problems. The trouble was, if you felt that way, you couldn't do anything to correct the situation. His grandmother had said: "You make your own way, *noozhishe.* You choose your path. Don't think you can accuse others of hurting you. You hurt because you choose to be hurt."

He remembered his grandmother's advice as he drove to his home in Scarborough. Scarborough hadn't been his first choice of a place to live. Not that there was anything wrong with it; it was just that in his mind he had always dreamed of a home to the north of Toronto, where the landscape was more rugged, the ground held snow in the winter, and his grandmother's cottage was only a short driving distance away.

The last visit had only proved to him how much he revered her place. Although grandmother had her own children and other grandchildren, it had always been understood that he would inherit the cottage. He never knew why. That it was a special place, he was well aware. That it had something to do with what his grandmother felt was his spirituality, he also knew. Yet, he wasn't all that sure that was the whole reason. He didn't notice anything special about himself. His grandmother was definitely biased in that regard.

Jade had really felt at peace in the cottage, and his grandmother had accepted her as part of her family already. He didn't even bother to wonder why. It had to be something other than Jade's looks, for with her blond hair, green eyes, and her tall legginess, she certainly didn't fit anyone's stereotype of an Ojibway. He acknowledged that his grandmother accepted her and let it go at that. If he never saw Jade again, he doubted very much if she would visit the area of his grandmother's house by herself, and it was almost a certainty that she would not go to her aunt's cottage again. A stab of pain pierced his heart.

In the intervening weeks between his return to Toronto and his trip to North Bay for the trial, Jason received a letter. It wasn't wholly a surprise to get home one day and find a letter from his grandmother in his mailbox. She wrote occasionally, more, he thought, to get a reply from him than to tell him any news from home. For extremely important matters or emergencies, she would telephone.

He thought of her fondly as he tore open the envelope. Her written words surprised him, yet as he thought about what she had written, he knew he agreed with her one hundred percent. There was no bitterness, no regrets. He could telephone his grandmother now with his assurance of his accordance with her decision, but he preferred to visit in person.

If this was his grandmother's ploy to get him up north, it was certainly working. He was so elated about the turn of events that he couldn't wait for the trial before he traveled north. He looked forward to the coming weekend.

Friday evening found him turning in at the special place he had called home for so many years. After the hectic weeks in the city, he felt himself relax. His tension had slowly worked itself out of his system as he drove and left entirely when he entered the drive. His grandmother was sitting comfortably in her favorite armchair in front of the open fireplace he had helped to build. The night was warm with just a slight damp chill; the fire was small, enough to ease the dampness out of the cottage back into the night. Peacefulness was always the hallmark of the small house, even more so tonight when he was happy and troubled at the same time.

"*Noozhishe*," she smiled at him now, with the love of years of tending him. "You are troubled, but it will soon pass."

He looked at her doubtfully, for the first time unwilling to believe in her deep faith and far-seeing eyes. "I've come to stay the night, Grandmother." He tried to sound hearty and carefree, but the effect was strained. There were too many memories of his last visit here with Jade.

"I may not be able to come any more, but I want you to know that I agree with your decision. I have no regrets. You have loved me well all these years, and I have appreciated your love and strength. You took care of me when you should have been able to rest from raising children. You have given me more, Grandmother, than many people get in a lifetime. I want you to know that I'm happy with your decision."

She smiled at him. "I'm glad. There are not many more days or nights in this world when the two of us may visit like this." She touched his arm briefly, knowing that when she spoke of things like this, he became uneasy. "You must not be afraid to say the things you believe. Others may laugh at you, but if you believe in yourself you will come out winning and smiling. Now," she said briskly, changing the topic, "Tell me about that lovely young Jade of yours."

"There is nothing to tell," Jason informed her warily. "And she is certainly not *my* Jade." He wasn't all that sure that his grandmother didn't have inside intelligence on what was going on in his life anyway. She seemed to get a lot of information from somewhere. "We haven't seen each other since we returned to Toronto. We thought it best that we go our separate ways. After all, life is not the same when it becomes routine. When you're living on the edge, as we were for those few days, everyday things aren't important anymore. Customs and habits and rules and regulations of society are meaningless. Sometimes it's easier to love in those circumstances than in everyday situations." Looking at his grandmother, he felt that his whole monologue had passed over her head.

"You're still on the outs and choosing to be hurt, is that it?" She gave him a wry smile. "Does she know how the case is going? Does she know that she's been scrubbed as an accomplice?"

He burst out laughing at his grandmother's uncanny ability to use the jargon of his trade and to know precisely what was going on with his work. She was a great woman at adapting to circumstances, and he only hoped that he would have half her courage and resilience. He grinned at her now, as the truth of her statement sank in. She had always had a way of seeing through, around, and over any rationalization that he had come up with.

He couldn't remember ever having told Grandmother any of this about the case, but maybe he had, when he had telephoned her in such a turmoil, or maybe she had gleaned the information from Tom. He knew that Tom had a soft spot for his grandmother, though the man would never admit it. Whether or not he had told Jade, he couldn't remember, either. He said as much to his grandmother now.

"Why don't you drop by her apartment to tell her how the case is progressing from your side," Grandmother suggested.

Jason frowned. He couldn't see what good that would do. After all, Jade must know something of what was going on just from her Aunt Kate. He had also heard that she had paid a visit to Derek to set him straight about proper relationships, ending with the ominous words: "I hope you never get married, or find anyone with whom you'll fall in love, then you will know what it's like to never have anyone you trust."

She had left Derek sitting red-faced in his office as she stomped out of the building, oblivious to the others in the station. Thankful that he had not been on the receiving end of her tirade, Jason had silently applauded her action. He had thought for a while that he might go to Derek and commiserate with him. But then he decided that Derek could hold his own. After all, he had done quite well when Jason himself had frothed over him in his anger.

He might just take his grandmother's advice, though, he mused the next morning on his way back to Toronto. He had five hours from Marten River in which to argue with himself whether to go to see Jade or not. It was almost like pulling the petals from a daisy--should he, should he not? By the time he reached the outskirts of Toronto, the matter was more or less wrested from his hands when he found himself turning automatically onto Stellar Avenue at a detour sign erected by the summer construction crew.

He had never been to Jade's house, but knew her address from files. She lived in a good suburb in a beautiful, large house. The police files had listed her as living in the basement apartment. He girded up his loins for the confrontation.

In the seven weeks that had elapsed, Jade had tried to get some semblance of order back into her life. But order was always being preempted by some new event that arose. The first was the visit from Aunt Kate. Flying in from her Florida condo, as she had said she would, Kate had picked up her car from the airport parking lot and driven out to Jade's apartment. She greeted the worn and tired Jade with a maternal smile and hug, as always. It was Jade who pulled back from the embrace. She had looked at her aunt. "You knew," she whispered, aghast. "You knew about Rick's activities, didn't you?"

Her aunt looked startled. Kate had hesitated, but then seemed to sense that Jade would settle for nothing less than the truth. "May I have a cup of coffee?" she had asked diffidently. "It would help."

Jade knew she couldn't *not* offer her aunt hospitality, not after all the years that she had run to her for comfort. She poured the coffee as her aunt began to talk about Rick. "But I never suspected that he would try to kill you, Jade. Never that," she whispered. She stopped abruptly, and Jade, seeing the tears in her aunt's eyes, found herself for once giving comfort to her aunt.

"Oh, Aunt Kate, I don't know what to say. You've always been the one who helped me and accepted me. I thought my cousins had accepted me, too. I never knew that Rick bore such animosity towards me."

"I didn't either," Aunt Kate sniffed, tears rolling down her cheeks. "He covered it very well. I'm sure the others didn't suspect anything either. But Jade, if I had known for certain, I would have turned him in myself, I swear it. As it was, I suspected that he was into drugs when I found some once on a visit to the cottage. The cottage hadn't been broken into, so I knew that it must have been either you or Rick, and for a long time, I suspected you."

Jade was shocked. "Me?" she managed to get out, turning a dismayed face to her aunt.

Kate nodded. "Jade, think about it. You had such a rotten childhood. Rick, I thought, had a good one. I didn't suspect him at first." She looked at Jade pleadingly. "He's my son, Jade. When you are a mother, maybe you will understand."

Jade thought she understood some things now. As long as it was drugs, the mother was willing to close her eyes to the truth about her son. She could see that Aunt Kate did not think drug dealing was such a serious crime. Kate had never allowed herself to acknowledge all the ramifications. Maybe there was guilt there too, Jade thought, a small doubt, perhaps, that she hadn't been astute enough to see through her son's early problems. Jade didn't know. She did know, however, that Aunt Kate was not smuggling drugs from Florida or trafficking in them and that she had not known about the murder of the young girl whom Rick and Len had mistaken for Jade.

Kate had been informed of some of the details by the police when they had telephoned her in Florida. She still wasn't clear about everything and, Jade conjectured, probably never would be. As a mother she would still go on believing that somewhere she had failed her son, whether she had or not. "You do see, don't you," Jade had said to her aunt, "that I don't want to ever return to your cottage?"

Kate had nodded, well aware of the break in their relationship. "If only Rick had known that you had turned down the cottage before, I wonder if he would have acted as he did?"

Jade didn't bother to answer, for the question seemed to call for no answer. It was speculation and part of the process of Kate's taking the blame on her own shoulders. Yet Jade couldn't fault her for that.

If it had been Jade, she knew that her aunt would have protected her too. She hadn't said as much, but it was implicit in the statement that Kate had made when she admitted that she had thought for a time that the drugs might have belonged to Jade. She had neither questioned

Jade nor turned the drugs over to the authorities, and Jade had to love her for that--even if Kate's logic was skewed.

Jade said good-by to her aunt, knowing that it would be some time before they would be able to speak to each other again on the same easy terms that had been the mark of their relationship over the years. They might see each other at the trial, but whether or not they would speak would have to be seen. Jade felt more alone than she had felt in years. She had lost her aunt as her confidante, but it seemed doubly troublesome now because she had also lost Jason. She felt more insecure than she had ever felt in her life. With Rick and Len in custody and the business with Derek cleared up, she should have felt calm, if not totally great.

After Aunt Kate's short visit, Jade began to use the book shop and her writing to fill the void in her life. It was not until three weeks afterwards that she found herself coming down with flu-like symptoms. One morning she awoke feeling lethargic and nauseated. It was all she could do to drag herself to work. For the rest of that day she had subsisted on coffee, able to keep nothing else on her stomach. As her symptoms dragged on, so did she. It was Bernie, old, wise, Bernie, who looked at her with a discerning eye and said gruffly, "Sure you're not pregnant, Kid?"

Jade felt the breath leave her with a suddenness that made her grasp for something to hold onto. Never had she thought of the possibility that the lovemaking she and Jason had indulged in would lead to this. She looked at Bernie aghast. His old eyes had seen life in too many of its strange twists to be upset by Jade's condition. She ended up telling him what had happened in the north. He patted her shoulder, made her lie down on a small cot in the back of the store and brought her a cup of tea, telling her in his droll manner to drink it slowly. "I don't want you upchucking all over my books and papers." Jade tried to appreciate his humor and concern, but somehow she didn't feel up to it.

It was only after she had taken a taxi home, an expense that she never would have considered in the past, that she had time to think over the possibilities of Bernie's astute question. She made an appointment with her doctor as soon as she arrived home, telling the receptionist that no, it was not about her scalp wound, but that she thought she needed a complete check-up after her ordeal. She hoped that would quell any speculation as to why an otherwise healthy woman would be asking for a doctor's appointment as soon as possible. She knew there were pregnancy kits available, but suspecting that Bernie might be right, she knew she would have to see the doctor sooner or later.

She made herself a cup of tea and ate dry crackers--another of Bernie's suggestions. Then she wrapped herself in a blanket on her couch and forced herself to think of the wilderness of complexities that being pregnant would engender.

She spent the night alternating between sobs and smiles. She had never thought she would ever want a baby. Even when she was with Derek she had never thought past the fond embraces. Now she considered the ramifications of abortion.

This would cost money that she could ill afford. Except for a small legacy that she had from the sale of her parents' house, which she had been very carefully husbanding over the past few years, she had nothing but her small salary from the book shop and the few dollars that her freelance writing brought in. These totaled enough to pay for rent, groceries, and utility bills, with enough left over to pay tuition for university courses on a part-time basis. Sometimes she had a few dollars left over to indulge herself, but luxuries were limited.

Her car had been bought when she had first sold the

house, and had been kept in excellent condition up to now by the garage mechanic three blocks away from her apartment who had a soft spot for her and was always hoping that she would give in to his constant demands for a date. Well, her being pregnant would stop that, she was sure. She couldn't see herself parting with the much-loved red sports car, but chided herself for her materialistic attitude: Which did she need more, the car or the money? She had rationalized that it would be no benefit to sell the car. The money she would get for it wouldn't go far, and then she would have nothing.

Adoption? Could she give birth to a child and willingly give it up? Jade thought that this would be the best option; yet, all her life there had been no one on whom to lavish her love. But was this a good environment for a child? She was wise enough to realize that she could do the child more harm by keeping it. After the fiasco of her own childhood and now the disaster of Rick, she wondered if it was such a good idea to keep a child. The one person she never thought of in all of these scenarios, which she forced to march through her brain until the small hours of the morning, was Jason.

Not for an instant did she blame him for her predicament, nor did she think of him as a means of support. She knew she could appeal to welfare, but had seen welfare mothers and their children. It was a continuously revolving circle. The welfare system, while purporting to help people get off welfare and back on their feet, more often than not kept them at the bottom of society. People then developed a "welfare mentality," which took tremendous courage and willpower to overcome.

She wondered if she would be able to keep her job at the book shop. She was not overly concerned about her writing. That could be done anywhere. As dawn broke over the horizon, Jade dropped into an exhausted sleep, determined that whatever might come, she would do all in her power to keep the baby--a boy, she was sure. It was only when she was drifting into a much-needed rest that the vision of Jason's grandmother floated before her.

Tell him, my child. This is my great-grandchild you are carrying. Would you deny him his rightful heritage?

Jade drifted into slumber murmuring, "No, Grandmother, you are right."

It had not taken long for the doctor to confirm her pregnancy. Giving her a vitamin/mineral supplement and assurance that her nausea would gradually subside, he began to question her marital and financial status. On learning that she was single and not about to divulge the name of the baby's father, he also did tests for H.I.V. and venereal diseases. Jade found this most embarrassing. Never had she been placed in such a position. Even when she had been grilled by the vice squad, she had not been as exposed nor had her pride attacked so viciously.

It was Bernie who set her priorities straight. "Do you want to raise an abnormal or sick baby?" He knew she did not, but knew that Jade had not considered the question at all. Having seen her daily for the past several years, he knew she had not been free with her sexual favors, but who was to say that this Jason guy had not? Bernie had prodded her a little more: "Have you considered asking this guy for support?"

"In all honesty, Bernie, Jason did not have to twist my arm. I was more than willing to take part." Even now, nearly two months after the fact, Jade's eyes assumed a dreamy, glowing luster.

Bernie looked at her in mock exasperation. "Women!"

She smiled and got up enough nerve to ask him, "Why did you never marry, Bernie?" Bernie, for all his loving care of her, was never forthcoming about his own life.

"I did," he told her now, succinctly. "That's how I know about women." He patted her shoulder, saying he had to wait on a customer.

Jade knew that would be all that she would get out of him. Bernie had told her that she could work for as long as she was able and then come back after the baby was born. She had made up her mind to do more freelance writing. She had not made up her mind yet to contact Jason. What would he say? One momentary lapse and the girl suspected of being an accomplice in a drug ring and the cousin of a suspected murderer was carrying Jason's child! Even though she had been cleared, a fact she had elicited from her militant march to Derek's office, she felt that Jason still harbored doubts about her.

Still, throughout the day, the picture of Jason's grandmother floated in her mind. Jade could almost see the old woman's face in her peripheral vision, pleading with her. *This is my great-grandchild; you must not forestall his destiny.*

It was while she was at home worrying over all the responsibilities that impending motherhood had thrust upon her that Jason rang the doorbell of her apartment. It took a minute for Jade to focus on the incessant ringing. She hadn't contacted any of her old friends in Toronto since her return, and answered the bell now with barely concealed curiosity. "Jason!" she gulped, trying to order her features not to betray any emotion.

"May I come in for a minute? I won't stay long," he promised uneasily when she showed no signs of letting him past the security chain on the door.

Nodding her head in the affirmative, she unlatched the chain and led him into her apartment. His tall six-foot frame looked ludicrous in her tiny room. She still had not said anything more after her initial outburst. Feeling shy and vulnerable, she whispered, "I'm not feeling well, so if you don't mind, your visit will have to be brief." She heard the quaver in her voice and hoped he hadn't noticed.

Even as she said it, she knew she wanted him to stay and

go at the same time. Yet she felt that if he did stay she wouldn't be able to help telling him of the baby, and she didn't want that--not yet. This was her problem and she would deal with it.

As it turned out, Jason really was in a hurry; she sensed that he was edgy and wanted to leave as quickly as possible. When he told her about the case so that she would know what was going on, she felt his relief when she informed him that she knew quite a bit about it already. His sigh was quite audible when he found out he wouldn't have to stay to answer any questions she may have had.

She wanted to ask about his grandmother, but couldn't get past the wall he had erected around himself. She knew, too, that he was having difficulty getting through her defensive barrier. Neither was willing to lower the defenses each had set up against the other.

They were apprehensive with each other, and it was with mutual relief that after fifteen minutes he said that he had better leave.

He hadn't said anything about the cottage. He felt that was his grandmother's prerogative. He hadn't said half the things he had wanted to say to her, he castigated himself as he drove away. So much for taking his grandmother's advice.

When she was subpoenaed to appear in court as a witness in the trial of Len, Jade looked forward to the trip north with both elation and apprehension. It had been three months since the episode with Len and Rick. Rick's trial for drug trafficking had taken place first. For his trial, Jade had not been called. She figured both Derek and Jason had something to do with that. Derek, out of a sense of guilt and Jason, well, because he was Jason. That Rick had hit Jade over the head was immaterial to the case. There were no witnesses to the assault, and even Jade had not seen her assailant.

For Len's trial, however, Jade's testimony was important, if not crucial. Although he had admitted to Jade that he had killed the girl, it still came down to his word against hers. The lawyers for both men had done their jobs well. Even though both Rick and Len had admitted their guilt to Jason, the admission was not permitted in court. In the preliminary hearing, both men had pleaded not guilty to the charges against them. At this trial, Len was being charged with attempted manslaughter of Jason, and Rick was being charged as an accessory.

Bernie was worried about her traveling alone, but she allayed his fears by telling him she would travel when the highway was free of heavy traffic. She would be careful, she had added for good measure.

"After all, I'm going to be a mother, and mothers look after their babies, don't they?" She thought of Aunt Kate, who had protected Rick from the law for as long as she could.

CHAPTER TEN

Jade wasn't any further ahead with her problems now than she had been four months before when she had motored this north highway, but she certainly wasn't in the same blind panic she had been in then. In fact, she felt more comfortable with herself and with her life now. True, there was a hollowness somewhere inside that she couldn't fill with her dedication to her work. Only Jason could do that. On the other hand, there was Jason's baby occupying a small part of that hollow, and that compensated for much.

Jade was happy to be on the highway, car windows open, feeling the cooling breezes finger her hair. Late summer was drawing to a close, and already the trees north of Huntsville were beginning to put on the reds and golds of their autumn dress. Huntsville seemed to be the boundary between Southern and Northern Ontario, although she knew that people in Southern Ontario would dispute her opinion. As far as they were concerned, north was anywhere just north of Toronto. North Bay might be a barren wilderness of ice and snow, and Marten River and beyond were No-Man's Land. Jade knew better, for it was in the Marten River area, *No Man's Land*, that she had found the life-sustaining love she had been seeking.

In the four months since her return to Toronto, so many things had happened for her to think about. Bernie was the only one who knew about her baby. She hadn't told her aunt nor had she told Jason. Because she was naturally slim, she was only beginning to show slightly, and she could hide that under her suit. She would have to face Jason at the trial; whether she would tell him then, she didn't know. It all depended on his reaction to her. He hadn't phoned to ask about her travel plans to the north. Neither had Aunt Kate, but she had expected that. When Jason had visited her in her apartment, he had asked if she would need a ride. She had turned him down at the time for many reasons, but the overriding one was that she was afraid to be with him for any length of time. She trusted him implicitly, but she didn't trust herself.

Jade let her thoughts wander to the countryside that she loved. Even the bush, so tangled with overgrowth and dangerous swamps, could not repel her. Always from now on, whenever she thought of the northern bush, she would think of the tall, handsome Indian who had led her through the dense growth to safety just when she was on the verge of giving in to her delirium and fever. Whether he was a figment of her imagination or not, she didn't know, but somehow, she knew he was linked to Jason and his grandmother. Whether or not she and Jason ever did get together, she had made up her mind to see his grandmother, out of love, and out of a need to seek answers to her many questions.

She traveled slowly, savoring the heady stillness of the waiting world of late summer. Through the open windows, she could smell the fresh pine scent that permeated the north in every season, and reminded her now of the fresh sheets in the old woman's home. The intermittent rank stench of the open bogs and swampy land could not dampen her enthusiasm. They were not pleasant, but were an integral part of the undeveloped northern bush. It was like living in a steel smelting town, or in parts of New Zealand where the sulfur permeated the air. The odor became such a natural part of the place that after a short time one didn't even notice it.

Crows and ravens croaked their raspy greetings and

gathered in their nesting aeries high in the top branches of closely-growing poplar trees. Once she glimpsed a deer, its white tail visible through the thick growth, bolting into the bush to hide from her passing car. She glanced at a rather deflated porcupine along the highway, not so lucky in its attempt to get close to civilization. When a raven swooped down to pick at what was left of the strewn flesh, Jade felt a tremor of apprehension snake through her. After the trial would she, like that porcupine, be helpless against the swoop of predators?

She bypassed Powassan and Callander along the new stretch of highway. Nearing the ramp for Highway 11B, she turned off. After driving for two kilometers, she found a *Best Western* just on the southern outskirts of North Bay. She had made a reservation in advance. With the highly-esteemed restaurant on the main floor at the back, Jade knew that she would have easy access to meals. Now that she was past the nausea stage of her pregnancy, she constantly craved food. Over the next little while, she would become the restaurant's most frequent guest.

The trial was being held in the new red brick courthouse in the older part of town, with which Jade was only slightly familiar. She hoped the proceedings would not last too long and that she would soon get to visit with Jason's grandmother. Bernie had been more than generous about giving her time off, but she didn't want to take advantage of his good nature. She would have to work as hard and as long as she could while she still could. However generous Bernie was, he certainly wasn't going to pay her while she was off work, and she needed to earn as much as possible.

Bernie had insisted that she continue to take courses at the university. "It can't hurt. Education never goes to waste," he had told her. "Educate a woman and you educate a family."

She had heard that before somewhere. Bernie was fond of coming up with appropriate maxims, she thought now with a giggle, as she checked herself into her room.

Sighing with relief and stretching her cramped limbs, she drew herself a bath, careful not to let the water run hot, as she usually preferred. Not taking any chances that she might harm the new life within her, she compromised with warm and added a generous helping of lemon balm herbal bath oil to the water.

The fragrance brought back memories of the mint Jason had used to freshen their bodies after their lovemaking. Just thinking about it, she found herself becoming aroused. Lord, here she was already pregnant, Jade chided herself, and she was still eager for a romp with the man if she could get it.

She soaked in the tub for half an hour, getting all the cramps from the long drive out of her limbs. She studied the thickening of her waist and abdomen. Her breasts had already become softer and her nipples had darkened with pregnancy, but other than that, Jade was sure there was nothing that could give away her cherished secret yet.

She had brought a tailored pale blue suit with her for the trial, and now ruminated over the fact that Jason had seen her only in jeans--and in the nude. In fact, now that she thought of it, he had seen her at her very worst, with welts, bruises, cuts and all. Anything else would be considerably better. She felt she was looking her best, and knew that her pregnancy had given her face a subtle glow.

Her sleep was long and deep, far longer than she had expected. She wasn't as yet anxious about the trial, or about what she would say. Even having to face Len didn't bother her. Any animosity toward either him or Rick was gone. She could think only of the hurt that her aunt must be suffering.

It wasn't until she arrived at the courthouse the next morning that she realized the parents of the murdered girl would be at the trial, and she felt a pang of guilt that their daughter had been mistaken for her.

Jason found her in the hall outside the courtroom door. He stopped short. Lord, she was more beautiful than he remembered. Her pale blue outfit deepened the green of her eyes. She wore her white-blond hair coiled on her neck, and her skin, glowing with a natural pink color, held an aura of mystery.

He hesitated, wondering if he should speak to her, but it was a moment's hesitation only. Nothing or no one could keep him from her. He strode purposively toward her. "Hello, Jade."

As he touched her arm she felt a tremor of delight weave its way through her body. She had difficulty breathing. He was stunning in a dark grey suit with a stark white shirt and dark red tie. "Jason," she whispered almost shyly. "You shouldn't be seen with me."

His face took on a perplexed frown. "What do you mean? You know you've been cleared of any complicity. Also, to anyone not familiar with the case, it's simply a matter of a man talking to a lovely woman."

"You shouldn't be seen with me, " she repeated. "These people know about my relationship with Derek and they know I'm related to Rick. It will ruin your reputation and your testimony."

Jason felt his mouth go dry. He could barely manage to get out his next question. "Is that what this is all about?" he queried her. "You're worried about my reputation? I should have listened to Grandmother." He drew his lips together in self-disgust, as Jade stood before him, brushing the tears from her face. He noticed that people were beginning to stare at them, but he didn't care. He was near tears himself. "We can't talk here. Meet me afterward. Please," he begged. "I love you. Believe that, even if you believe nothing else."

She entered the courtroom tentatively, feeling intimidated by the oak benches and stark white walls. It was the same feeling she got whenever she entered a church. In fact, now that she allowed the thought into her mind, there was much similarity between the courtroom and a church, and she wondered if there had been a deliberate attempt on the part of the justice system to create the same ambience. You felt guilty even if you couldn't remember why.

She craned her neck to look at the number of people in the courtroom. Some looked as apprehensive as she; some looked as though they knew all the idiosyncracies of the courtroom and court procedure. Probably they were courtroom groupies. She speculated briefly whether lawyers had groupies following them, just as stars did. She supposed some must. There were people who got off on courtroom drama as others did on rock stars.

"All rise!" The bailiff's voice lifted above the whispered conversation of the spectators. "The people versus Leonard Doberman. The Honorable Judge Lytton presiding."

There was rustling and coughing as the people reseated themselves. Jade could sense the myriad emotions throughout the room. Some people were completely relaxed, probably in the room as spectators. She was reminded of the picnics and gaiety shown at beheadings and hangings in old books. Some were merely curious; a few were ill at ease. She suspected she was among the latter group. The trial began.

It turned out to be a nightmare. Jade was allowed to stay in court for the first day, but after that she would have to wait in an annex until she was called. Jason was called first. He stated how and why he had been in the area to begin with. His testimony was brief and germane. The cross-examining lawyer asked to recall Jason at a later time. Court was adjourned. Two days later it was Jade's turn. She related that she had been in the area for a holiday.

There was no sense in going into too much detail if she didn't have to. She told of the episode in the cottage when she had sustained her wound. Knowing it could not be called evidence, she felt it nevertheless lent some more credence to Jason and Tom's testimony. As Jade was forced to relive the events when Rick and Len had been searching for her, she had to keep requesting a drink of water for her dry throat and hoped fervently that her nausea, brought on by nervous exhaustion, would subside. She would be more than a little embarrassed, if she upchucked all over the court room.

At that point, the judge interrupted. "Miss Morgan, do you feel well enough to continue?" His fatherly voice held sympathy and was almost Jade's undoing.

"I'm all right, thank you." She sipped at her glass of water and forced herself to a calmness she had difficulty retaining.

The trial dragged on for days. Derek testified that they had put Jade under surveillance, hoping that she could provide them with information. This still upset her. The thought that she had ever been suspect hurt beyond anything that she had ever undergone before.

Derek pointed out that Jade had been cleared of any involvement with the two men. Jade conjectured whether Derek had bribed the lawyer to let him say that. She wouldn't put it past any of them. Derek had trouble meeting her gaze when she looked at him in the stand. He was ashamed and guilty. But she couldn't entirely fault his actions, either. Like Jason, he was a professional doing his job. She had to keep reminding herself of that or she would hate all police officers for the rest of her life, especially Derek and Jason.

Several members from the Toronto headquarters testified. Jade was acquainted with most of them, and knew that it would be a long time before she would feel at ease with any of them again.

When Jason was recalled, he gave expert testimony as to his part in the case, telling the court how Tom had asked him to the area--off-duty--to help investigate the homicide. He said little about Jade, and she wondered if, because he was trying to circumvent anything that might incriminate her, his words came across to the court as weak and unbelievable. But the courtroom was quiet as he spoke in his commanding voice. His reputation coupled with his air of authority made the jurors sit up and take notice.

The trial was in its fifth day. Always in the back of her mind, to keep her going, was the thought of Jason's baby. She hadn't told the court about how she had found his grandmother, other than that she had stumbled upon his grandmother's cottage while she had been foundering about in the woods trying to stay hidden from her predators. She wondered how she could explain an Indian guide helping her through the bush when that guide appeared to be nonexistent. Jason hadn't understood Jade's allusion to the native and Jason's grandmother would say nothing about him to Jason, only that the time would come when they would know.

When Jade was recalled, she felt the need for discretion, without actually lying. She certainly didn't need the judge or the jury thinking she was mentally unbalanced and prone to having visions and hearing voices, she thought mockingly. Jason's grandmother was not required to attend the trial. Jade knew that the beautiful old lady had lived through countless trying times, and this would be just one more for her to wade through. She would have come if she had been called. But the court saw to it that her appearance would not be required. Instead she had sent a written letter explaining how Jade had appeared at her house.

Forcing her mind to concentrate on the proceedings, she listened attentively as Grandmother's statement was read out in the courtroom. The Indian woman had written that

Jade had shown up at her door and she had tended to the girl's multiple wounds.

When the lawyers had questioned Jade about her relationship with Derek, she glanced toward her aunt. She hadn't told Kate anything about her association with him. From the look on her aunt's face, it seemed to have come as a surprise that Jade had been a suspect from the beginning.

Finally, after ten days, the trial was over. The jury deliberated only a few minutes before they brought in a verdict: Guilty of aggravated assault, guilty of possession for the purpose of trafficking.

As yet, there was no real hard evidence to convict either of them of the murder of the girl. In the courtroom Jade turned her eyes to the parents of the murdered girl. The couple looked to be in their fifties or early sixties, hardy prairie stock. Both had silver hair and clear complexions, but their faces were drawn. She wanted to console them, commiserate with them. What could she say to alleviate their hurt and stress? "I'm sorry I wasn't where the murderer thought I was?" There had been no justice for them at this trial.

She wondered why they had bothered to fly out from their retirement home in Vancouver. Had somebody told them the murderer of their daughter had been found? Except for the out-of-court confession to Jason, nothing else had been said about the murder. Had there been a leak from the police to the press? Had the police, thinking they had a good case against the two men, contacted them?

Jade felt a profound sorrow for the unknown couple. Even more sorrow than she felt for her aunt. Regardless of the outcome, at least there had been some resolution for her aunt and her cousins. For the murdered girl's parents, there was still a loose end. There was to be no closure for them that day. Somehow Jade didn't think her condolences to the couple would ring true in any event. If she were in their place, she wouldn't want the girl who was supposed to have been killed offering sympathy. She felt exhausted and limp, her pale features attesting that this had been a drain on her inner resources.

Derek was pushing his way through the crowded corridor toward her, but she turned away. As she did, she noticed Jason talking to her aunt, but couldn't muster the energy to walk over to speak to either of them. She craved nothing more than to crawl into her warm motel bed. Tomorrow she would go to Jason's grandmother. It would likely be the last time she would see the old woman, for she would have no reason to travel north--no cottage, no getaway.

She felt an attachment to the native grandmother that defied the short length of time they had known each other, just as there had been an affinity between Jason and herself. She felt an hysterical chuckle start to bubble within her. Some affinity! That ephemeral connection was going to produce a child. Derek at last pushed and elbowed his way to her side.

"Jade." He wet his lips nervously as he gave her a piercing look. "What can I say?"

She shook her head tiredly. "It's all right, Derek. It doesn't matter." She hadn't known until that time just how true that was. "I have to go now. I'm tired. Maybe I'll see you in Toronto."

Derek hesitated and then backed away. He didn't like the strain on her pale face and went after Jason to tell him how exhausted Jade looked. Regardless of what Jade might think of him, he did have some finer feelings for her.

Jason, however, had already noticed her. He hurried to catch up with her just as she was getting behind the wheel of her car. "Get any tickets for speeding on your way up?" he teased her, trying to hide his own overwrought state. When she looked at him, she had to force her weary mind to make some sense out of what he was saying. The attempt failed. Her face was white and expressionless. Opening her door, he grabbed her arm and hauled her unceremoniously out of the driver's seat. "Get in the other side," he directed. "I'm driving you wherever you're going--and don't even think about arguing." She did as he requested. He slipped into the vacated seat and wheeled her car out of the parking lot.

When they reached the motel, he went with Jade to her room, where he poured himself a drink from the mini bar. This was one time he was sure his grandmother would agree with his having a stiff drink. He offered Jade a drink, but she shook her head, causing him to raise his eyebrows at her and give her a more discerning scrutiny. She looked totally drained, and he wondered if this was the time to force a confrontation.

"Jade, we need to talk, but this isn't a good time, is it?" he asked, putting his arms about her.

She shook her head.

She was withdrawing, holding something from him, Jason knew. She tried several times to say something to him, but each time stopped short of actually saying anything.

"Jade, whatever happens," he whispered, "whatever you feel for me, please know this. I love you."

She looked at him, her lackluster eyes beginning to shine again. "I love you, too," she whispered. "But I didn't think you would have anything to do with me. I don't want to ruin your career. You've worked so hard to get where you are."

Her words were his undoing. What she said was true. But he was to blame, not her. He knew the rules of his profession better than anyone. He crushed her to him. "Jade?" He buried his face in her long, thick hair. So much for his good intentions about starting over without the sex, he thought.

She nodded. But as he gently slipped off her clothes,

leaving a trail of kisses along her neck, her shoulders, her breasts, her arms, he noticed her deep fatigue and was reluctant to go any further. As his eyes moved back to her breasts again, he noted that they had darkened somewhat from when he had kissed them last, in the dappled sunlight in the glen. Perhaps the lighting in the motel room was more subdued, he reflected. He inhaled deeply and held his breath. Mastering his impulses, he placed her between the sheets and gave her a light kiss on the cheek. She was asleep within seconds.

For a few moments he stood looking down at her sleeping form, trying to decide how to fill his time. He should return to his own room at *Journeys End* at the other end of town, but couldn't get past his inertia. He was held captive by the completely exhausted woman in the bed. Tom had left immediately after the trial, and Jason guessed he had rushed straight home to tell Lorraine the outcome. Even if he had left the courthouse at the same time, he wouldn't have arrived home yet to Tilden Lake, so there was no sense phoning him. Jason decided to phone his grandmother to let her know that he would be staying in town for another night.

He had promised her he would go up to see her when the trial was over. Now she would have to wait for a few hours. Knowing his grandmother, he knew she would forgive him. Reluctant to disturb Jade's much-needed rest, he stepped out into the lobby to telephone. As he knew she would, his grandmother insisted that he stay with Jade.

When he returned to her room, he stretched out on the black faux-leather couch, his feet coming to rest on the arm, and tried to sleep. He wasn't very successful, so that when Jade started to call out and toss about in the bed in the early hours of the morning, Jason was at her side in seconds. Gathering her in his arms, he tried to soothe away whatever fears were lurking in her overwrought mind.

"Jason?" Jade's voice was drowsy "Are you still here?"

Before waiting for an answer, she pleaded, "Make love to me."

"Are you sure, honey?" His voice was husky with desire.

She nodded, sounding more alert. "I need you."

They made love tenderly, her hands caressing his head and neck, her fingers stroking down his spine. When he kissed her and stroked her tender thighs, her stomach muscles responded. As he gently massaged her stomach, she thought she felt the baby respond to his father's loving, and wondered if it was too early for that. She lifted her hips closer to him, desiring more, and pleading with him to take her.

Jason needed no urging. He was more than ready, and figured he was keeping himself under admirable control. He fumbled in his pocket for a condom, wondering why he hadn't used one the first time they had made love. Finally he could wait no longer and thrust inside her, more aggressive than he had intended.

Jade involuntarily jerked away from him, startling both of them. "Be careful, please, Jason," she urged.

He was baffled, but continued to pulse slowly within her as she arched her back to get even closer to him. When at last Jade uttered a cry of release, Jason let himself go and joined her in the bliss they had been missing for over four months.

In the afterglow of their lovemaking, she snuggled under his arm with her head on his chest as he lay on his back staring with a frown at the ceiling. After a few moments in which he tried to master his emotions, he turned to her. Grasping her under her arms, he sat her up facing him. "Tell me," he commanded her now. It had suddenly dawned on him what Jade had tried to tell him. He had put together the changes in her breasts and body and her startled urge for him to be gentle.

Jade looked at him and knew that she could not conceal

her condition any longer. With no dissembling, she said defiantly, "I'm pregnant." She looked at his furious expression and rushed on. "I'm not expecting you to support us or anything. I think we can get by." She went on to explain her plans to him.

"Were you ever going to tell me?" He addressed her now with controlled fury. Never in all his years had he wanted to shake some sense into a woman as much as he wanted to shake her. He wondered how he could be so in love with her and feel such rage at the same time.

"I dreamed your grandmother told me to tell you," she told him quietly. Somehow she didn't feel hesitant about telling him of her visions, especially as they pertained to his grandmother.

He looked at her now, with a mixture of wrath and love and tenderness. "Did you think I wouldn't own up to being the father?"

She shook her head. That was the one thing she had never thought of. She knew that she had been with no man other than Jason, and accepted as fact that he knew that too. It was only when Jason questioned her, that she realized there could have been other men after him. But there hadn't and she was sure that Jason was aware that he had been her only lover.

He hugged her again. "I'm more to blame than you are, if there is to be any blame," he added. "I just assumed that all girls today were on the pill. That you could be a virgin never crossed my mind. Plus, I've been feeling guilty as hell because I didn't use a condom. I, of all people, should have known not to have unprotected sex! I'll get tested as soon as we get back to Toronto."

"Jason, you don't think you have anything, do you?" She held her breath, waiting for his answer.

"No. I'm absolutely sure I don't. But, we have to be on the safe side. I'm assuming you had tests?"

She nodded. "I was terribly embarrassed, but Bernie set

me straight on my thinking."

He looked at his watch. "Come on, get dressed and we'll go down to the restaurant for breakfast. I hear it's quite good, and I'm starved. And you should be too--unless, of course, you have morning sickness." He added the last as a half-question.

She smiled happily. "I seem to be over that nasty condition. That means we'll probably have a son, if all the old wives' tales are true." He appeared to be happy about her revelation, she noted. Her observation was confirmed a moment later.

"By the way," he stopped her momentarily as they left her room. "I don't think there should be any blame. I'm proud to be the father of our baby. Are you happy about it?"

At this point she was able to nod an affirmative. "I wasn't at first. I was terribly upset, but now I'm beginning to feel quite maternal."

After a leisurely breakfast, at which Jade made up for the missing meals of the last few days, they checked her out of the motel.

They had to retrieve Jason's car from the courthouse parking lot, as he needed to stop off at the OPP station to see Tom before going to his grandmother's.

Jade chose, irrespective of Jason's wishes, to travel independently in her own car. It was only then that Jason realized he was still dealing with an independent woman used to doing her own thing and having mostly her own way. He wondered how he would cope with that. It also occurred to him that they would have to travel back to Toronto separately to get both their cars back there. The prospect did not appeal to him at all.

"Jade." He was suddenly quiet and intense. "You drive my car back to Toronto tomorrow."

"No." She was adamant. "I'll be careful, Jason. I know I'm protecting our baby now." She hugged his arm.

"Besides," she cajoled, "don't think for one minute that I will let you drive my car. You would probably drive it well over the speed limit."

The drive from North Bay to Marten River usually took thirty-five minutes. Jade arrived about an hour before Jason, so she had time to ask his grandmother some of the questions bothering her. By the time Jason arrived, they had only a short time left to spend at the cottage.

Jason proudly told his grandmother about the baby, but Jade knew the old woman was already aware of it, even though Jade hadn't told her. Jade didn't get a chance to ask her all the questions she longed to ask. She was shy in front of Jason about saying too many things that might seem weird to other people. She knew his grandmother understood about her visions, but she wasn't sure just how much Jason understood. She was also curious about the cottage and her vision of the woman. The old woman patted her arm, sensing the many unasked questions.

"It is all right, my child. There will be time. I must come to your wedding," she added pointedly. "What should I wear, I wonder?"

Jade and Jason both started in surprise. Neither had even thought of getting married, although that would have been the logical train of thought in more ultra conservative couples, Jason thought.

Grandmother shook her head at them in mock disgust. "You are getting married," she emphasized. "None of this modern stuff about living together. Do I have to come to Toronto for your wedding?"

Without thinking, both answered, "No." Each knew that the other wanted to get married where they had met. Now they sat talking over their new plans with Grandmother. Their city friends would not mind coming north for the wedding, especially in the lovely mid-October weather, the time they settled on for the ceremony that would seal their love. Both thought it did not matter to them whether or not they were married, but out of deference to his grandmother, they both agreed they should do it--and promptly. In return they asked only that his grandmother come dressed in native dress.

*

There were no blackflies or mosquitoes. The lakes were still and serene, waiting for the icy blasts to freeze them into an enforced rest. The trees held onto their leaves of red, yellow, and russet, reluctant to let go of their vibrant party dress. The contrast to the white birch bark and the dark pine needles added to the collage of colors.

Jason and Jade married in North Bay at the beautiful old Pro Cathedral. Grandmother was serenely happy. She stood out amongst their other guests, for she wore a soft velvety deerskin outfit from years past. It could have clearly outshone even the bride's dress, but it did not. Grandmother had insisted that Jade wear her own bridal dress, now sixty-five years old. Jade had no parents and nothing handed down from her family, so Grandmother did not have to worry about hurting anyone's feelings. "Think of it as the dawn of new traditions," she said in her soft voice. "You and Jason are the beginning of the next part of this world."

The dress had been hung lovingly and carefully in a closet, with no folds allowed to mar its beauty. It was butter-soft white deerskin, carefully and lovingly crafted by Grandmother's grandmother. The beading and quills still retained their original luster. The whole ensemble was breathtaking. Jade had doubts at first. She wasn't a virgin, she reminded Jason's grandmother, and therefore should not wear white.

But Grandmother had set her straight about that. Those were man-made customs, she told Jade. In fact, it was Queen Victoria who had started the custom of wearing white wedding gowns. Before that, the bride could wear anything. And, she added, gazing pointedly at Jade. "If it

still bothers you, just remember it is Jason you are
marrying and you were a virgin before Jason."

"How do you know?" Jade asked, laughingly, only
slightly curious.

"Women know these things. Now put it on. You will
have to wear your own shoes, as your feet are too big for
my moccasins."

On her head Jade wore a veil held in place with a comb
of orange blossoms, Jean's contribution to the bride. When
Jean had seen Grandmother's cottage, she had known in an
instant it was the one Jade had dreamed about all her life.
"As consolation," she had told Jade, "I expect an invitation
to your wedding, as I have missed out on my commission
for finding you a cottage."

"It is not my cottage, but you're quite right in saying
that it's what I've been looking for. And, you will
definitely be at our wedding. In fact, I would like you to be
my matron of honor," Jade told a delighted Jean.

"Not being native, or anywhere close to it, would it be
all right to wear a dress more in keeping with my own
tastes?"

Jade had agreed and Jean wore a soft shade of bluish
grey that brought out the russet highlights of her hair.

Their friends had indeed not minded at all traveling the
four hours from Toronto on the special bus that Jason had
provided for the event. Jade had not realized that Jason
had a legacy from his Scottish grandparents. His Indian
grandmother had held it in trust for him for years until he
came of age, but even after that he had not touched it,
wanting to make his own way in the world. Now, for this
extra-special occasion, he used some of it to pay for the
wedding. He had hired a bus and driver to maneuver their
friends from Toronto to North Bay and back again the next
day. For the evening, he had provided them with motel
rooms.

The guests were herded into the bus for a tour of North

Bay's waterfront, with its famous carousel, the Lavase Heritage Park and a trip to the hill overlooking the city and Lake Nipissing. In the evening they were treated to a play put on by the Nipissing Stage Company. By the time of the wedding, all the guests were in a party mood.

Jade had prevailed upon her aunt and cousins to attend the wedding. Aunt Kate was reluctant to attend, but as she, along with her daughters, was Jade's only close relative, she accepted her niece's invitation. Jade had glanced over to them at one point and noticed Jason and Tom making her aunt feel welcome and at home. Her cousins were adept at making friends on their own.

Their reception, a casual lawn party with a local band, a Scottish piper and a trio of natives with their drum brought choruses of oohs and aahs from their more conservative guests. Jade doubted that any of them had been to a wedding with such a mix of traditions.

Later, the newly married couple traveled to Jason's grandmother's vacated cottage, his grandmother having chosen to stay with one of her own children for the week. She had stopped them just before they left the reception. "This is my special wedding gift for Jade."

She had already given them a lovely set of china, and had lent Jade the deerskin wedding dress, so Jade was mystified, although she noted that Jason was smiling and knew he was aware of the special gift.

As his grandmother handed Jade an envelope bearing the name of a firm of solicitors, she placed her hand on Jade's arm and said, "I want you to know that I would have given this to you, even if you hadn't married my grandson. Jason has known about it for a long time." Jade opened the envelope. Inside was the deed to Grandmother's cottage, with Jade's name as owner.

Jade felt the tears trickling down her cheeks. "But, Grandmother," she protested, "we will be living in Toronto for most of the year. It will be a shame to let your beautiful home go idle for so much of the time. And besides, it shouldn't go to me. Please, if you don't want to give it to Jason, give it to one of your own children or another grandchild."

Grandmother smiled and shook her head. "It won't go idle. It's a home of love. Love has soaked into the very fibers of the wood and into the grounds. Look on it as a legacy to my special great-grandchild."

Jade nodded. She understood Grandmother's meaning.

"And where love is," Grandmother continued, "there is never emptiness. Enjoy yourselves for this week. I will be back. You don't have the cottage yet, you know. I'm not quite ready to begin my journey to my next world."

Jade and Jason spent an idyllic week at the cottage. It was even warm enough one day to make love again by the stream. The leaves fell quickly now, and the water was too cold for them to bathe in afterward, but the blue jays darted back and forth among the leaves, and black squirrels and striped chipmunks dashed about, gathering acorns and seeds for the coming winter. Goldenrod grew at the edge of the glade, and the dark red torches of the staghorn sumac glowed as beacons for the migrating birds. Everything lay in wait for the chill to follow. But Jade and Jason felt nothing but warmth, the love from the cottage, the embrace of the glen, the heat of their love.

The week ended all too soon, and again they made the return trip to the south. They had moved all Jade's furniture into Jason's Scarborough house, and had prepared one of the rooms as a nursery. One day Jason took her along to the office to see Derek. They had invited him to the wedding, but he had begged off, saying he had other plans. Jason felt that Derek had been a little in love with Jade himself and probably still felt more than a modicum of guilt at his handling of the situation. He had sent them a lovely gift, though, a hand-carved and inlaid coffee table, and they had invited him to the cottage the following summer. They judged that by then, enough time would have elapsed to put all the events of the recent past into perspective.

When they saw him now, he was his usual gregarious self.

"Hey, guys, look at this," he offered. Another police officer was toying with a computer makeup kit and was aging the faces of children who had disappeared several years previously. "Hold still," he teased Jade, "and I'll show you what you'll look like when you're an old lady. I have a photo of you from a few months ago." He didn't have to remind her that the photo was one he had taken when she was smitten with him. It took several minutes for him to do the aging. Jade looked at it transfixed. It was the woman of her vision. Images started to jell, her vision began to slide, and she saw herself talking to the woman in the vision, the woman who had been a widow. Jade stifled a sob and ran from the room.

Derek looked after her, startled. "Jason, what's wrong?"

As Jason chased after Jade, he assured a contrite Derek that the outburst was probably caused by a change in her hormones. He didn't let on that he was terribly upset himself. "Honey." He had caught up with her on the sidewalk and stroked her hair. "It's all right." She was trembling with shock. Jason rushed her into the car, wondering if he should take her to the hospital. She was now six and a half months pregnant, and he didn't want anything to happen. "Jade, honey, please think of the baby. You don't want to have it too soon," he begged.

Jade breathed deeply, forcing herself to calm down, and nodded her head. "I have to--to see your grandmother," she hiccupped into his shirt.

"Jade, be reasonable, honey." He knew that it was the wrong word to choose the minute he said it. She glared at him, angrily.

As they arrived home, Jason was still trying to reason with her. "The roads, Jade. You know what they're like in this weather. Honey, please. What is it that you want to see Grandmother about? Please, can't you just talk to me?"

She considered for several minutes in silence. She didn't want to agree with Jason, but she also knew that the road conditions were very uncertain at that time of the year. She could fly to North Bay, but even that took effort, and she would still have to get from North Bay to Marten River.

After deliberate and measured breathing, sitting on a golden beige couch in their living room, she had herself under control and began to tell him of her visions, not only of the cottage, which she had touched on before, but about the many times throughout her life when she had visions. His grandmother understood her, she told him.

Jason nodded. "Would you believe me if I told you that I understand, too?" he asked her gently.

She was beginning to shake her head in disbelief when she looked at him with dawning recognition that he did understand her. But as she sat there, the tears began again in earnest. She didn't want to tell him of this particular vision, but finally he coaxed it out of her.

"What is it about this particular vision that's bothering you?"

She glared at him angrily, wondering how one man, who was supposedly such a marvelous detective, could be so bloody obtuse. "I'm a widow," she yelled at him. "Don't you know what that means?"

Jason thought back over the whole vision as she had explained it to him. He left her on the couch, where she had sunk in her misery when they arrived home, and went to fetch a note pad and pencil. "Look," he explained patiently. "Were you ever any good at mathematics or even arithmetic?" he teased. "How old did you say the woman in the vision was?"

"About eighty-seven," she replied.

"And how long did she tell you she had been widowed?"

Jade looked at him. She had forgotten that detail, but was sure that it was there in the back of her mind somewhere. Her mind had just registered that she had been a widow. After delving into her memory, she managed to dredge up the tiny but important bit of information. "Three years," she told him.

"How old does that make you when you become a widow?" he urged.

She wondered for a moment if he knew he was acting like a police sergeant grilling a suspect. She began to laugh, but there was also a sob in her voice. "Jason, I don't want to lose you."

"Darling, after all that time, you probably will want to be rid of me," he teased. He tried to lighten her mood but found it almost impossible. "Jade, honey, we can't live indefinitely. We live the best we can for as long as we have. If you are widowed at eighty-four, that means that we will have been married for fifty-eight years. I'll be ninety-four when I die. That's a hell of a lot longer than many people get, my love. Don't live in the future, my darling. We'll live out our destinies as we can. He hesitated; he was beginning to sound more like his grandmother every day. A glowing pride arose in him and Jade noticed it. She smiled.

"You'll take your grandmother's place yet, Wise One," she laughed. "But not yet, please. Right now, I need the love that only a special man can give me."

He complied.

EPILOGUE

Sean Michael entered this world in early March, along with the birth of a new spring. Named after Jason's two grandfathers, he was born with his mother's straight moon-blond Nordic hair and the promise of his father's dark obsidian eyes. He was a boy, Jade insisted with maternal pride, destined to break many hearts before he found his true love. Jason was inclined to agree.

Over the previous months they had been forced to cope not only with moving, but also with adjusting to each other's needs and moods. With the strain of Jade's pregnancy adding to their period of adjustment, they hadn't visited his grandmother over the Christmas holidays, but they had telephoned her at her son's house. Shortly after the Christmas season, Jason's beloved grandmother had died.

Jade wondered why she didn't feel more heartbroken. Jason was subdued, but that was only natural, Jade knew. After all, his grandmother had raised him and loved him well. When Jade told Jason that she wanted to take their son to their cottage as soon as possible, he happily agreed.

Two months after Sean Michael made his appearance, the new family drove to Marten River. The spring had been mild, and the red and white trilliums were blooming in the woods; fern fronds were shooting their green spears out of the damp earth, eager for a new season. Along the cleared glade of the cottage, the Oriental poppies had rocketed out of the brown earth with a burst of riotous red and orange, and the green lawn was flourishing in the warm spring rains. The stream burbled rapidly, swollen with the runoff of the melted snows that were now feeding the budding trees.

Robins had returned to build their nests in the pines and the maples. The cedar waxwings plundered the mountain ash berries from the summer before, leaving scatterings for the evening and pine grosbeaks, who needed the fruit to build up their strength for nest building. Pine siskins and warblers flitted about, intent on establishing their territory. As the world was awakening to give birth to a new season, Jade smiled, languorously content with her own new motherhood.

She did feel a slight disappointment but tried to cover it. The homecoming she had anticipated, showing her new son to Grandmother, would not take place. She unlocked the door, which swung open on well-oiled hinges.

Although they had told no one they were coming that weekend, the cottage smelled fresh and gave them a feeling of vibrancy, yet Jade knew that no one had been in to open it up and air it out.

She grinned at Jason. "I'll make a pot of coffee. You show your new son the beautiful stream where he will play and fish for brook trout, and the field where he was conceived," she added playfully.

He laughed at her. "Shall I tell him all that?"

"Hmm, maybe you'd better omit that part. If he takes after his father, he will find out soon enough." She was learning to live one day at a time. "Take therefore no thought for the morrow . . . " may have come from the Bible, but she was discovering that the philosophy was found in many peoples' beliefs and deserved at least some of her consideration.

Laughing heartily, Jason took the baby outside into the sunshine. Already the cottage was working its magic. Jade felt better than she had in years and knew that Jason felt the same. It wasn't all the cottage, of course, but it had played a large part in their love, which was deepening each day.

A few minutes later, Jade, holding a fresh cup of coffee, gazed through the large living room window that overlooked the lawn and the stream. Jason was showing Sean Michael to a beautiful young Ojibway woman, dressed in the deerskin clothing of years past. She was smiling down at the baby and saying something to the Indian man at her side. He nodded in agreement.

The man, wearing the same deerskin clothing, was the one who had led Jade to safety through the bush the summer before. Looking content and happy, they were linked arm-in-arm, gazing lovingly at the baby boy and saying something to Jason who held his blanket-wrapped son snuggled in his arms. As the Indian couple turned to leave, they glanced back at the window where Jade stood watching. Both the man and the woman smiled in recognition and love, and Jade could have sworn the man winked. As Jade stood watching, she distinctly heard them both say, "*Onizhishi*, he is nice, our great-grandson."

Jason beamed with pride and turned toward the cottage, and the man and woman hovered above the stream and disappeared into an early spring mist.

Source for Ojibwe words:

Nichols, John, and Earl Nyholm, eds. <u>An Ojibwe Word Resource Book</u>. Minnesota: Minnesota Archaeological Society. 1979.

Ambe: "come!" "attention!" particle

mawadishiwe: "he visits" animate intransitive verb

nindikwem: "my wife" independent animate noun

nookomis: "my grandmother" dependent animate noun

noozhishe: "my grandchild" dependent animate noun

onizhishi: "he is nice" animate intransitive verb

By Carol A. Tipler:

THE STORYTELLER AND HIS STORY
Early in the 21st century, the earth is destroyed by a series of meteor hits. An alien race which has been monitoring the planet has chosen one woman to become the Allwisemother of humankind. This is her story and the story of her descendants who retell of the birth of the new world.

GENTLE ANNIE
She came from the Aboriginal Dreamtime to help her beloved in his dreaming. In pre-history northern Australia, Mpwartwe, Coober Pedy and post World War ll Alice Springs, Annie has to be tough to fulfil her role. In between her incarnations, she returns to the Dreamtime, where she becomes her natural self and dances and sings with the MD, Python, and Unicorn.

By the same author, under the name of **Anne Ravenoak**

THE RETURNING
He had loved her a century ago, when she was a young Irish orphan sent to live with her cruel distant cousin in Cornwall. He was a valet to that cousin in Ravenhall, the family home. Their love could not be. They reincarnate in this life to experience their love and to bring closure to many unfinished relationships.

SECRETS OF THE BLUEBIRD INN
If you liked Marten River Hideaway, you will love this second book in the Marten River trilogy.

An angel, her work finished,
Tossed a soft kiss to the world
And slipped quietly home.

ISBN 1-41206074-5